LOVE GIVE US ONE DEATH

LOVE GIVE US ONE DEATH

Bonnie and Clyde in the Last Days

A novel by

JEFF P. JONES

Texas Review Press
Huntsville, Texas

FIRST EDITION

Requests for permission to acknowledge material from this work should be sent to:

Permissions
Texas Review Press
English Department
Sam Houston State University
Huntsville, TX 77341-2146

ACKNOWLEDGMENTS
Troy Knighten's reminiscence is taken from Patrick M. McConal's book *Over the Wall*; Emma Parker's reminiscence is taken from Jan I. Fortune's book *Fugitives*; both are used with permission of Eakin Press. Lee Simmons's reminiscence is from his memoir *Assignment Huntsville* and is used with permission of the University of Texas Press. W. D. Jones's interview is taken from *Playboy*. Ted Hinton's reminiscences are taken from his book with Larry Grove, *Ambush*. "Old Hannah" is from John A. Lomax's *Adventures of a Ballad Hunter*. More particular source information is noted in the Afterword.

My thanks to the Texas State Library and Archives; the Texas Prison Museum; the Dallas Public Library; the Texas Ranger Hall of Fame and Museum; the Bonnie and Clyde Ambush Museum; the University of Idaho Library; the MacDowell Colony; Gavin Ross and Loic Zimmermann; Lindsey Alexander; Mary Clearman Blew, Dan Orozco, Joy Passanante, Rochelle Smith, Alexandra Teague, Cynthia Wong, and Robert Wrigley; Mike and Meg Andrews; and Gary Williams. Deepest thanks to Jane. In memory of William Cook, April O'Brion, and Paula Jones.

Cover image: "Bonnie and Clyde." Courtesy of Loic Zimmermann.
Cover design: Nancy Parsons

Library of Congress Cataloging-in-Publication Data
Names: Jones, Jeff P., 1972- author.
Title: Love give us one death / Jeff P. Jones.
Description: First edition. | Huntsville, Texas : Texas Review Press, [2016]
Identifiers: LCCN 2016015972| ISBN 9781680030976 (pbk. : alk. paper) | ISBN 9781680030983 (e-book)
Subjects: LCSH: Parker, Bonnie, 1910-1934--Fiction. | Barrow, Clyde, 1909-1934--Fiction. | Criminals--United States--Fiction. | GSAFD: Biographical fiction.
Classification: LCC PS3610.O62568 L68 2016 | DDC 813/.6--dc23
LC record available at https://lccn.loc.gov/2016015972

for Jane

LOVE GIVE US ONE DEATH

Bonnie and Clyde in the Last Days

An engine of more than forty horsepower
annihilates the old morality.

Viktor Shklovsky

You've read the story of Jesse James—
Of how he lived and died;
If you're still in need
Of something to read
Here's the story of Bonnie and Clyde.

Bonnie Parker

1

LOVE'S KINGDOM

May 23rd

In the early days of their courtship, there opened a piney hallway not unlike this one, a strip of oil road in the backwoods of east Texas along which Clyde had been pushing the car faster and faster, trying to scare her by topping blind hills in the oncoming lane and lifting two wheels on the curves and thudding them back down on the straightaways, and even as she felt the fear colonizing her throat she sensed a deeper urge, and what she did was this: she peeled her fingers from the dash and, grabbing the sill, thrust herself out the window to the waist, and the figurehead she became— half machine, half woman—spewed hellborn laughter into the battering lovely slipstream.

January 5th, 1930

To escape the Bog in West Dallas, Clyde's father Henry moved their scrapwood shack to a lot that fronted onto a gravel thoroughfare. The place suffered a constant plague of fumes and dust. The address was 1620 Eagle Ford Road. *H. B. BARROW* was burned into a crateslat nailed over the canopy under which red gas went for ten cents a gallon, white for twelve. But the whole point of the enterprise was the tacked on oil room in back, where Henry kept smudged business papers, a hodgepodge of tools, and three ten gallon kegs of low grade whiskey. Each keg took a cupful of Dr Pepper syrup and was catalyzed with an electric needle. The popskull was sold out of the station and from Henry's fetchit wagon, where he kept Coke bottles stoppered with paper plugs in a secret compartment under the seat.

When an errant driver struck and killed the family gray, a court ordered the man to buy Henry a pickup truck to restore his livelihood. This was shortly after the failed robbery in Denton during which Clyde's older brother Buck had been shot through the knees by officers and arrested. Clyde, having made his getaway on foot, latched himself in the back room and refused to leave. Inside that closeted space, he constellated wood knots and nails, followed the woozy flight of a bluebottle fly as it thwapped the walls, and listened to the outdoor sounds that trickled in, the sudden rain of children's feet or men murmuring around a crackling barrel fire.

One twilight, his mother rapped on the door. Cumie Barrow was an old farm wife who'd borne seven children. "Come and get you a bite to eat."

"Aint hungry."

"My foot. I got fatback soup out here. You feeling peaked?"

"Couldn't say."

The door creaked as she put her weight against it. "How long you going to sit around like a notch on a stick, son?"

"At least one more minute."

"Get out and get going is what I say, mister. Quit being so resty."

When a skulking shadow emerged from the Eagle Ford shack into the brown haze of dusk, it wandered the city like a detached spirit, weaving between crowds and passing stores and cafes in which people smiled and joked with each other. It slipped down streets with wet leaves sticking to its brogans. It swallowed the meatless sandwiches and watery soup handed out at Salvation Army trucks like it was a chore. The shadow moved in holiday gloom with an unfocused gleam in its eyes, clouting through rain showers and even a light snowfall. Sights passed by, but it paid no heed: magnificent rows of electric lights, diamond patterns of inlaid red brick on a storefront, painted window signs advertising *5¢ Doughnuts* and *Fresh Coffee*.

The shadow plodded ahead and entered a neighborhood. The rain fell in lines of silver, then ran down the shadow's face in streaks of gray. This was the hour when the houses turned to spectacle, the stages of home life glowing in amber rectangles. It paused to watch a family take supper. The children sat upright in their chairs as the mother leaned over the father's bowl and ladled his portion first, then each of their bowls in turn, and hers last. The father's spindly neck looked too weak for his head. He joined hands with the children on either side of him and closed his eyes.

The shadow scowled and walked on.

It passed acres of cramped houses in silent rows. One had all its windows broken, another, a black ribbon hanging from the door handle. The shadow's clothes grew soggy, its lungs tightened, a fever frosted its skin. An icy mantle enveloped its brain. Something was wrong, but it couldn't be approached directly. The shadow was headed somewhere and when it stepped onto the viaduct, the row of electric parapet lamps shone on a wiry young man whose hands were stored in the pockets of a mud colored suit coat and whose stare cut the ground. He was halfway across the viaduct when something drew him to the concrete railing. He leaned on his forearms and peered over.

To the east rose the city with its soaring white buildings, its constant hum, its lights and motion, while to the west spilled a dark swath dotted with the tents and farm wagons of cotton refugees, themselves gray specks squatting beside wet fires. Bats teemed where a moment ago had been rain. The breeze carried foul smells, combusted gasoline and smelted metals, and under those, an empaneling of rotten fish, burning tires, boiled greens.

Below, separating the city's two halves, was the river, a silky black ribbon whose surface held a smattering of reflected lights. Cold spite crept its fingers up his legs, his back, his shoulders. There was a purity, an icy clarity, in its touch, and he released himself into its grip and loathed of the viaduct with its hissing cars and loathed of the river's glittering. He despised every miserable acquiescing soul. He hated the rich and he hated the poor, and it was a mark of distinction that he was able to keep his hates separate.

At the corner of Ross and Market, he passed the old city jail with its upper story windows encased by bars. *Texas Ice And Cold Storage* stood out in letters as white as the moon. He swiveled away from an intersection where an officer was directing traffic and went down another street. To reach the police station, which was inside the county courthouse, he had to go straight for three blocks then turn right, but, with no forethought, after the second block he turned left and aimed toward Main.

At Akard, an interurban rumbled by, the airish faces in the windows aglow with light, all of them except the coloreds in back looking like members of a royal lineage. The city roared in his eardrums. The faces flashed past. He reached for the lights, but they swam away. Darkness closed in. He was alone, trembling and cold with sickness, invisible. An instant before he was struck by a passing car, someone seized his arm. A voice called from behind.

"Watch yourself!"

Then laughter, and traffic flowing around him.

"Probably some plowboy from Oklahoma."

Someone had his arm and was pulling him back to the curb. He looked for whoever it was who'd laughed, saw only a jumble of faces jostling and gaping. One face in particular was looking straight into his.

"Clyde Barrow, what's gotten into you?"

It was Ernie McLuhan, a West Dallas kid whose folks lived on Willomet. They hadn't set eyes on each other for months. Not long ago, they used to run in the same group that horsed around at Fair Park, taking photo booth snapshots and chucking acorns at spooning couples. Ernie wore the crisp khakis of a filling station jerk and had on a dark wool jacket, checkered, and a cap so shiny that it flashed in the light. His face was filled with friendly magnanimity. When Clyde didn't answer, Ernie suggested coffee and guided him past a newsstand, where copies of *Collier's* and *Life* were suspended slaunchways from hooks.

The cafe was spacious and clean, with a long counter at which sat a sole diner finishing a slice of ham, his nose in a newspaper. A headline read *Hoover Predicts Spring Revival*. A couple sharing a soda at a window table whispered conspiratorially. Ernie hung his jacket by the door and chose two counter stools.

"You seen the paper?" Clyde asked.

"Can't say that I have. I just finished my shift."

"Say, would you grab one? I'm busted."

Ernie's face darkened. He forced a laugh and went out to the newsstand. By the time he returned, he'd settled into dignified gloating. He slapped Clyde's shoulder and set the folded paper at his elbow. "Don't fret, the muddy waters are on me."

Clyde opened and arranged the paper with a great deal of noise before slipping into embittered regard, mumbling over its contents. "Hell, is this what's called treacle? A fire broke out in a theater . . . another banker thought he was a bird . . . a man was struck and killed by a tram in front of the Adolphus—"

"Might've been you tonight, captain. That's one way to get your name in the headlines."

The waitress leaned backward when she poured their coffees, then set a server of milk before them. Clyde turned the page.

"What is it you're looking for?"

"My brother was to have been transferred this morning."

"Which one?"

"Buck."

"Where's he going?"

"Huntsville."

Ernie, grinning, shook his head and leaned his elbows on the counter. He added two seconds of milk to his cup, then held it with both hands under his chin, occasionally sipping. He spoke as if to the flash of himself in the counter mirror. "A real live prisoner for a brother. You must be swelled up with pride. What did they get him for this time?"

Clyde took in his old friend, glancing at the tiny black bow tie over his Adam's apple, then, lightning quick, flicked Ernie's collar before returning to the paper. "I wouldn't worry about it if I were you. After all, you've already got a stock in trade as a pump jockey. You feed people smiles and check oil for a living."

"You feeling all right?"

"Why, do I seem strange?"

"I oughtn't to give you a hard time. You look like you've took sick."

"What if I have?"

"Then let's get you on home. Let's us call your people."

"Aint no way *to* call em."

"Then I'll call someone else."

Clyde brought out a Coke bottle from inside his coat, uncorked it, and poured a portion of its contents into his coffee. The man eating his supper glowered. The waitress pretended not to notice. Clyde took a long swallow from the bottle before pocketing it, then turned to Ernie and gave him the full on. "Let me say this. It aint the way I expected things would turn out."

Ernie looked at Clyde's coat, the worn elbows, the frayed seams, the buttons hanging from a single thread. He circled the coffee cup, swallowed half of it down, then thrust his heels out from the stool. "You sound like this old sow at the station. Hates his job, his wife, the weather. That sort of sad sack gibbering can go to hell for all I care."

Clyde darted a look at Ernie, then leaned so close that his old friend could smell his sour breath, the hair oil pressing out from his scalp, could feel the heat tiding off his skin despite his shivering. "What if I told you I was there with Buck when they nabbed him? What if I told you it was my idea in the first place, that Denton job?"

"It's no business of mine," Ernie said and fished in his pocket for coins.

Clyde fell to whispering. "I done worse than that. That what you want to know?"

Ernie slipped off the stool. "What do you want to tell me that for?"

"Sit down. I've got more to say."

"You've lost it. You're just spewing burro milk."

"Sit down," Clyde said.

When Ernie complied, Clyde seized his arm as if he might pull it from its socket. The couple glanced over. The man at the counter reached for his wallet. The waitress fled into the back.

"Do you know where I'm headed? Don't you want to know? I'll tell you. You'll be the last one to see me." He dug his nails into Ernie's arm. A passing face paused at the window. "I'm going away."

Ernie grimaced. "Go on, if you like that. If it helps."

Clyde was reaching into his pocket when someone entered and approached. Clyde and Ernie looked up. It was Clarence Clay, another old confederate. He sported a watch chain dangling from the pocket of a tailored overcoat. Pomaded dark curls peeked out from under a fedora. He was smiling and approaching them in high humor.

"You two here together, what's the chances?" He shook both their hands eagerly. "Why, I'm glad I spotted you."

Clyde rolled the newspaper into a baton and tucked it under his arm.

"How the hell've you been?" Ernie asked.

"My sister's gone and broke her arm," Clarence said as if it were a happy thing. "It's this freeze up every night. Damn ice is slick as a whistle. I'm having a blow for her tonight. Why don't you two drop by?"

Clyde was detaching himself. Ernie addressed him in the mirror. "If you weren't so peckish, you should go. It would do you some good."

Clarence added, as if stumbling upon a favor he

could do, "It's the white box clapboard at Herbert and First. One oh five."

"I've made a decision," Clyde said, "and I'm sticking to it."

"His brother's been sent up," Ernie intimated behind a cupped hand.

This reportage flashed across Clyde's face as a melting of concern. He laughed, full and long, at how ridiculous he and Buck must've looked in that alleyway, heaving that safe into their trunk when the laws turned the corner and threw on their headlamps. He chucked Clarence in the shoulder. "Don't you worry none. Day by day in every way, I'm getting better and better."

This jingled Clarence, who said, "What's gotten into him?"

Ernie shook his head. "He's fixing to do something drastic. I think he's sick at the thought of it."

"What you need's some amusement," Clarence said.

Clyde went out, hands fumbling for his pockets, gaze rebounding.

"Hey there," Clarence called. He was holding the cafe door open. "Come on by. She'd appreciate it. We used to have high times."

"I'd sooner eat a wasp nest."

"What can it hurt?"

"I won't be there," Clyde said and moved into the sidewalk crowd.

As it turned out, he changed his mind.

The Stock Exchange and Commodity Exchange as operated today are not essential to conducting our commercialism, they are merely and truly LEECHES on a great commonwealth and should be EXTERMINATED. Sentiment, generally, at present favors the EXTERMINATION of these damnable leeches.

—Waxahachie resident to Texas Sen. Tom Connally, Nov. 26, 1929

In March 1929, Bonnie changed jobs, to Marco's Cafe. Whenever a customer swung open the door, in poured the rumble and stink of tractors clearing ground for a triple underpass and plaza that would eventually be named after the owner of the *Dallas Morning News,* George Dealey.

At Marco's, Bonnie was a customer favorite. She stood a sparrow's wingspan over four feet, weighed less than ninety pounds, and wore bobbed hair the color of a blond flame flickering into red. Bangs of thin rills veiled her forehead (her hair kinked into popcorn curls when wet), and her face dimpled on both cheeks. The men she served were enchanted with her spitfire ways, her worldly smile, her knife edged comebacks. She would waylay a wandering pinch with a pinch of her own. Her mind held an immense storehouse of trivial memories, and she could palaver with a stiff as easily as a high tone lawyer. She moved like quicksilver from one table to the next, pulling everyone into her circle and coloring her speech with unladylike words. When called to account for it, she said that she learned to swear at the age of three and had been so cute that her father refused to spank her, so she'd never been cured.

One of her regulars was Ted Hinton, a quiet man with a rugged face who worked at the nearby post office. She would deliver his pie and coffee with, "Here you are, Handsome," and regale him with details about her upcoming Broadway career. Then she might nod at some tramp in the window and disappear. A little while later the cook would holler and Bonnie would come out from the kitchen looking like a scolded puppy. She was risking her job to hand out kitchen scraps. In time, Hinton would be deputized by Sheriff Smoot Schmid, and in time Hinton would twice hold Bonnie in his rifle sights, but in 1929, as Texas enjoyed the end of a drought and its first healthy cotton crop in years, the cafe was boisterous. That summer and fall, Hinton and Bonnie saw each other several times a week.

Even when the stock market crashed in late October, the bulk of Texans—especially Dallas businessmen—believed the eastern calamity would merely erase paper profits and have little bearing on their newfound prosperity. The effects, though, were felt soon enough, and when Marco's closed in early December, Bonnie retreated to her mother's house and sank into Christmas doldrums. She ordered and reordered her closet, dyed her hair, glued runs in stockings, wore out the pages of the Sears Roebuck catalog.

The day after New Year's, a cold front blew in. Bonnie leaned against the sink and stared at the white spicules forming on the kitchen window. They crept across it like fine fingered roots. When Anna Lee Clay, a friend, stepped off her porch that morning, she slipped on a sidewalk rimed with ice and fractured her outstretched arm. For five dollars per week, Bonnie agreed to stay with Anna Lee as a helper. And on the first Friday after the accident, Anna Lee's brother Clarence surprised her by organizing a party of old friends to cheer her up.

Ted Hinton :

Bonnie was perky, with good looks and taffy-colored hair that showed a trace of red, and she had some freckles. She always had a ready quip, too. She must have been a good student, for she had won a spelling bee when she was in school. I couldn't imagine her having any criminal record; she was such a tiny girl— couldn't have weighed a hundred pounds. She had married a schooldays chum named Roy Thornton when she was just fifteen or sixteen, and they had parted over something or other. A little after that, Thornton was caught in a robbery and was sent to do some time in prison. Bonnie never did divorce him. She just said, "it wouldn't be right."

Several of the men my age flirted with her, and Bonnie could turn off the advances or lead a customer on with her easy conversation. I'm sure she must have been seeing Clyde on occasion at the cafe, but I have no memory of seeing the two of them together there.

The two teenagers were together in the tiny kitchen, Clyde at a spindly table, Bonnie orbiting around the stove. In the corner stood a battered wooden icebox. From the other side of the swinging door erupted voices and laughter.

Clyde was puzzling over the mystery before him. Her face was lovely, but he couldn't luxuriate in its full light. He hadn't gotten past her hands, which seemed to contain all of her, and which held the paradox of Bonnie Parker in all her petite ruggedness. They were tiny, the fingers as slim as pencils and the skin oiled and smooth, yet when she picked up the kettle or closed them around a cup, green veins piped around the bones and tendons sprang to the surface.

Then there was the ring she wore.

"Be careful, it's hot," she said and held out a steaming mug.

He wrapped both hands around the cup. Inhaled the steam threads. Then, he couldn't help himself, he reached out and caressed her hand, and the stiffness in his fingers registered the warm liveliness of hers, and something else. She acknowledged the breach with a smile and withdrew her hand. There was delicacy wed to strength in her face. Lively mouth. Aquiline nose. Warm but fleeting eyes that said she was keeping something back.

"My, your fingers are cold," she said.

He took a sip, felt the warmth flow through his icy shell.

"Sweet enough?"

"Never tasted better."

When she sat, the electric light overhead cast images of them in the panes of glass on either side, old selves keeping watch and nodding at times. She spoke in a fast stream, revealing that she was nineteen years old; had waitressed for the past two years; was free enough to call herself "damaged goods" as she flashed the thin wedding band ("I was young and head over heels, but I don't regret a thing"); and that her dreams went beyond the Dallas city limits. She'd lost her job a little more than a month ago. She dismissed it all with a wave, then leaned in and said, as if it were a question, "But I get so blue sometimes."

In the coming weeks, as he fretted away in a Waco jail, Clyde would often return to this night to dwell in these first impressions. Even the moment before he'd glanced at her was vivid in his mind. He'd been in the front room, propped against a side table, fighting a cold sleep, nodding off and half listening to Jimmy Leonard go on about some gun opera, when he gradually became aware of a curl of light swaying in the periphery. It rocked there like a tongue of flame in a breeze. Its rhythm of reach and recede soothed him. But the beguiling thread grew so bright, he knew it would pull his gaze, sensing all the while, even then, that looking its way would cost something. So he stalled, climbing the sweet rungs of possibility, considering, in some manner, what he had to lose, which in the end didn't seem like much. So he turned to look.

A woman the size of a girl. Red bobbed hair with finger waves and a pair of studded combs. She was talking with someone, standing with her arms crossed, right foot turned outward, feet shoulder width apart, and she was deploying her hips in a slow swivel that somehow suggested she had, in fact, grown aware of *him.*

All this in one glance: glowing skin and pretty face; a pared down beauty of muscular curves and concentrated movements; a readiness to engage with whatever came her way; sophistication and sentiment; and this, most intriguing of all, a devilmaycare hardiness seen only in those who refuse to be cowed by circumstance. He didn't even have to ask—this was no East Dallas girl, she was West side.

When they were introduced a few minutes later, she quipped about him being a banker, what with the newspaper tucked under his arm, and it was like reuniting with a childhood friend. In short order, she covered her preferences for red beans and cabbage, Camel cigarets, and Maybelline eyeliner. Her mortal fears were snakes and lightning. It wasn't just that he knew, from the start, he could show this girl everything about himself, it was that he wanted to. Her presence worked on him like a warm, welcome wind. It thawed his blood free of its frozen shores and flowed it upward, where it cracked the icy mantle over his brain. There were funny asides and proddings to be made, inquiries and teases, and all of it was fueled by a trepid hilarity that led to their laughing not at what was being said, but at how everything was suddenly, wonderfully alive.

She said he looked flushed and led him into the kitchen, where she retrieved a tin of cocoa powder from the pantry and lit a burner on the stove under a fire blackened kettle. He sat while she outlined her life. At one point, she leaned over and lit a cigaret off the burner. Her hair was lovely the way it curved around her ears. Then she was pouring streams of sugar into steaming cups, and now they were sipping their cocoas.

"You still married, then?"

She drew in a long breath through the body of her cigaret and exhaled a plume heavy with her feelings. "It seemed sort of dirty to divorce Roy once he was sent up. I just didn't have the heart for it."

He nodded. "You know, you've got what they call natural charm."

She smoothed her dress over her knee, clearly pleased. "That's what my third grade teacher said when she cast me in the school pageant. Mama shoeblacked my face and put a yarn wig on me. I was supposed to say, *'Ah kint haz inny kandy, mistuh, else my mammy'll tan mah hide'*"—here she clasped her hands and appealed to an adult—"but the class clown plucked off my wig and spoiled my performance. There I was in front of an auditorium full of parents with my costume blown and all that I'd prepared so hard for ruined. I started pounding that shoalbrain in front of God and everyone. The people, they loved it. After that, I just did what came natural, started jigging right there onstage and doing cartwheels. The show fell apart. The whole place liked to riot to see a little blondhaired pickaninny cutting the rug with tears rolling down her cheeks."

"You strike me as a born dramatist."

"You can ask anyone in my family, I've never been one to avoid the central spotlight."

"How come you haven't got fellas chasing you around the block?"

She looked at him from across a distant plain. "Who says I haven't?"

Clyde plucked his hat from off his knee and rotated it by the brim.

She said, "If there's anything you want to know about, you ought to ask me. I don't have time to beat around the bush with fellas anymore. Are you curious, for instance, to whom I gave my virginity?"

"Can't say that I'm not."

"It was to Roy a week before we were married. I lacked a month on my sweet sixteen."

"You were a holdout."

"Well, I waited so long because I wanted it to be with the man I loved. It may have been a schoolgirl's love, but it was love all the same."

"I'm glad to hear it was happy for you."

"If I had to guess, I'd say that you were an early bloomer."

Clyde donned his hat at a rakish angle for a joke, drawled, "You might say so," then doffed it again and spoke plainly. "Nah. I was just a hayseed on a farm till we moved to the Big D. Weren't long after coming here, though, I was arranging meet ups for local girls looking to cash in on their assets."

"My, you *were* a quick study."

"That soured me some on West Dallas girls."

"Just where do you think I call home?"

"You're as pretty as a picture."

"I know how things work, is all. I wasn't fishing for flattery. There were girls at the cafe who dated some of the customers. It was just another source of income."

"As long as we're being brutally honest, I wonder whether you weren't tempted the same."

Bonnie crushed the cigaret into a saucer, then sent a look that crackled and raced through him with Pentecostal heat and left behind a shiver. "Sixty hours a week my mama watches a needle jump on an endless piece of fabric, her elbows brushing the woman next to her. It's infernal hot in that sweat box, and the roar from all those machines is so loud she can't hear a shout. What she breathes aint properly called oxygen. She's given twenty minutes for lunch, but she can't go outside and see the blue sky or taste the fresh air. I keep a picture of her in a frame from when she was twenty, and we look like twins. I love my mama more than anything in this world, but I don't want to *be* her." Bonnie sat back and crossed her arms. "What if I did feel that temptation, what's it to you?"

Clyde said, "I've been arrested more times than I have fingers to count. You could name any town within a hundred miles of here and I've broken laws in it. You could throw me in a pool of holy water and I wouldn't get wet. I'm nineteen years old."

While she was still laughing, a wintry mood came over him. Without meaning to, he began telling her about the Dallas police, how they yanked him out of work each time there was a robbery so that he couldn't hold down a job, and then kept him for days sometimes, shoving a confession paper in front of him for crimes he didn't commit.

Bonnie shook her head.

Clyde went on. "A few months ago, they put these lights in my face, right up close so I couldn't see nothing behind them. Then they started hitting. Wham in the gut. Wham in the chest. Wham right in the kisser. I couldn't tell where the next shot was coming from. One of them bastards knocked me clean out, and I have no idea who it was. I woke up back in my cell with my head pounding."

"That's awful," she said.

Then he brightened. "Say, I want to show you something. Tell me if this aint jake." He pulled a pistol from his pocket and spun the trigger guard on his forefinger's hook. It came to rest aimed at his own reflection. He said, "Bang."

She shrieked.

A face peeped in at the door, then retreated.

Unfazed, he proffered it to her, handle first. "Go ahead."

Bonnie braced herself against the chair back. "My lands! What do you want with that thing?"

"This son of a bitch leapt clean out of my grip the first time I fired it. It's my thumb buster. Here, don't be afeared." He formed her hands around its grip.

But she shrank away. "No, thank you. Once, when I was a girl, I brushed my grandfather's iron while making his bed and liked to scream myself silly. Guns frighten me, they do."

"I'll tell you one thing I've discovered. People take a sudden interest when you show them the business end."

She busied herself lighting another cigaret as he bandied the gun from one hand to the other. He spoke as if to himself. "It's a funny world, aint it? Us against them."

She said, "You're sort of a wild card, Clyde Barrow. I never imagined that a boy such as you existed."

"May I ask you another question?"

"Yes, if you'll put that ugly thing away."

He spun the pistol again and slid it into his waistband. "What's something secret that nobody else knows about you?"

Her eyes traveled to the window. She needed a moment's reprieve from the changes occurring inside her, from her heart springing against her chest like a wild creature. *Why don't something happen?* she'd written in her diary not long ago. Now here something was, happening. She spoke in a voice that eddied and rushed. "I wish more than anything in the world to have a baby, but I'll never be able to. I don't talk about that with anyone because it makes me so sad. I could never have fathomed the depths of sorrow a person can feel before I lost the only baby that was meant to be mine. There are women who don't appreciate what a wonderful gift motherhood is. A child's squandered on such a person. If I could just have one little old baby, why, I'd love it to pieces."

Laughter floated in from the other room. She said, "Let me tell you this else that only my family and close friends know. I dye my hair so often, people sometimes don't believe that I'm an original blond, but I am."

"I could tell you were the first time I laid eyes on you, what with your fair skin and all."

"I freckle at the first hint of sunlight." When silence threatened to pool around that, she said, "Now it's my turn to ask you something."

"I'll tell you anything short of my shoe size."

"What is it you most want from life?"

He rocked the chair onto its hind legs and teetered there. "When we lived in the Bog, our home was a tent that we fixed to the wagon with a cord. That place aint proper ground, just a suck of mud that'll pull your shoes plumb off. Black flies hovering over thunder mugs. Mosquitoes as thick as smoke and each one a malaria needle. Babies wailing, kids trading the days they get to eat. Them mossbacks crush into that campground like feeder pigs, then they wait for the next charity wagon. They live like livestock and are happy to do it.

"Most nights I couldn't sleep a wink, so I'd sit on the buckboard and gaze across the river at that city behind glass. I'll tell you one thing, I aint going to wait around on no handouts. What I want's my share. The worst thing I can imagine is rolling over."

"The worst thing I can imagine," she said, "is being bored."

When it sounded like the others were about to spill in, he reached across the table and took one of her hands—and there it was again, a linkage, or perhaps only a fever addled perception of a linkage, that held ancient forces, light behind light, dark swallowing dark, terrible heat and withering cold. Her hand flitted like a trapped bird, light boned yet ready to strike, wanting to trust but wary of giving itself over to an encaging power. She pulled it back, but he went on, telling her how he'd expected to be in a jail cell or maybe the morgue instead of sitting there with her drinking hot chocolate, which made her laugh, and he moved out into the broader territory of his recent life, storying his criminal past: the car thefts, burglaries, getaways, and the near getaway in Denton; then he moved on to Buck and his predicament. Through it all there were no notes of braggadocio; he simply needed her to know these things as cleanly as possible.

And what did she think of the doings of a smalltime crook? Was it or wasn't it a better life than standing around with his teeth in his mouth?

He couldn't have spoken more directly to her. He expressed the precise fears and frustrations she felt, but up until then had yet to fix with names. He didn't have Roy's size or rough handsomeness—his face was softer and his ears jugged from the sides of his head—but he was good looking in a pleasant way. His dark hair was thick and nicely combed. His cheeks wore a red cast. His thin eyebrows perched atop puffy lids, and his gray eyes made him look as if at any moment he might ask a penetrating question. Even sick and unsettled, he was smarter and funnier than Roy and harbored a charm. This boy was too eager to be kept down. Just to be next to him would mean adventure.

In the time since Bonnie and Clyde roamed the country's byways, cosmologists have determined that the earth and everything on it is composed of the dust from disparate exploded stars, and from a certain corner of that field, one physicist, shunning approbation, has suggested that the attraction two people feel toward each other may be the result of sharing material from the same star, their very molecules pulling by undiscovered powers on each other. Whatever forces were at work the night of January 5, 1930, in Clarence Clay's kitchen in Dallas, Texas, what's certain is that by the time Clyde was tilting his cup and scrolling the chocolaty sludge across its bottom, Bonnie was growing cloudy eyed with romantic yearnings. When the door finally burst open and a gaggle of partygoers broke in, then fell into an embarrassed hush, the pair saw how ridiculous the world had been made. Their former pals were bozarks and bozos with faces acne ruined and nincompoopish. The kitchen had shrunk into a closet.

Chilled by the pair's bonded intensity, the others left in twos and threes until the house was nearly empty. Clyde mumbled something about taking his leave, but Bonnie pressed the back of her hand to his forehead and pursed her lips. "I won't allow you to travel, not like this. You'll stay on the davenport so's we can keep an eye on you."

He was led to the front room, where she helped him out of his jacket and dress shirt. His undershirt was gray with fever, and he was given one of Clarence's clean shirts, which was soft and dry against his skin. Bonnie pulled a quilt up to his chin, and he rested his head in the swallowing softness of a pillow that he recognized already as holding her smell: fresh cotton, warm skin. Then the world that harbored the flickering flame of this girl with the ring curls pinched shut, and the last thing he knew was the caress of weightless fingers on his arm before slipping below the surface to a place where he could at last sleep the sleep of the dead.

Clyde :

daddys grip on that dead
twin sack bare hands
dragging burr and blood

from can see to cant
mama embering the iron
with coals from the fire

killing centipedes
where they feed
on flour paste glued to tar

paper behind newsprint
us kids gunning redskins
with hip shots in the yard

while the wind whips
& the walls hiss

This guy, he'd get them out there in that field, and you wouldn't believe this, but what this guy would do is watch those men work; and he would undo his pants and just place his testicles right out there on top of that saddle. Then he'd pull out that frog sticker knife he'd always carry with him, and as those men chopped the weeds between the cotton rows this guy would slide that knife back and forth across his testicles, pulling off any chiggers or gnats or bugs that were on him. All morning long, he'd just slowly scrape his testicles with that frog sticker and he'd watch those men as they chopped cotton. Trust me, if one of those men got too slow, wouldn't keep up with that hoe line, he'd call them over there. Everybody knew that something was going to happen. They would come over and say, "Yes, Boss man?" He'd say, "Boy, pick up that stick," pointing down at the ground at something lying near by. Well, as this convict leaned over to pick up the stick, this guard would pull out his service revolver and shoot near the convict's head. Of course the convict jumps, not knowing what was going on. Well, then this guy would sit there for about five minutes screaming at the top of his lungs at this man, asking him why he jumped and what did he think he was doing staying behind the rest of that line. Asking him why he's so lazy.

Anyway, just another Eastham story. Thought you'd want to know.

—Troy Knighten

2

Civiliter Mortuus

May 23rd

Bonnie's worst nightmares always came in the dead of night. The windows would be pitch black and the car would be swaying and bumping along as she tossed in the passenger seat. Each sway would become a swerve, each rut a gunshot. Men in brim hats lifted guns to their shoulders and disappeared behind fiery blasts. There was a shattering, the sting of glass, then the drum of bullets.

She always escaped, to live on without Clyde like Blanche without Buck. And the dreams all ended the same—with the car slowing and the dust settling, she'd look over at Clyde in time to see a red wire unspool across his chin.

This time, she snapped awake and reached for his arm. There he was, sitting in blue dawnlight, giving her a slow grin, saying, "How was your nap, baby?" She combed down her hair with her fingers, and they chatted for a while. Both were still sleepy, so they decided to try for another hour.

The next time they woke, it was to bees buzzing over sandwich leftovers on the dash. The sun came through the branches and banded the tree trunks yellow, and, though the windows were down, there was no wind.

"There goes your breakfast," Bonnie said.

Clyde harrumphed and rolled to his other side. "There goes *your* breakfast."

After a time, they sat up. She tossed the sandwiches out the window. Then they got going. Stopped in Gibsland at Ma's Cafe for two more sandwiches because Clyde was sour about losing the food but even more sour about having lost touch with their cohort Henry Methvin yesterday. Henry had gone into a cafe in Shreveport and never come out. When a police cruiser rolled by, Clyde took off. They returned an hour later, but Henry was gone. The rendezvous point, in case of separation, was the Methvin family place outside of Gibsland. They'd driven there twice yesterday. The second time, Clyde threatened Henry's folks if he didn't show up this morning, and now they were headed to meet Old Man Methvin, who, it had been arranged, would have Henry with him.

There was almost no traffic on the country roads. They drove under a blue sky with a dry leaf rasping around inside the hood. A piece of straw had become caught under the windshield wiper arm and split in such a way that it looked like a tiny man dancing at the whim of the air currents. South of Gibsland the road cleaved. White slab tombstones flashed past. They entered a pineland bog out of which rose ancient gray trees with limbs scarved in green moss. They climbed a hill and came upon a pulpwood truck and two negro swampers riding atop the logs in back. Clyde risked a blind hilltop pass, roared up and overtook them. He recognized the driver and waved. Buddy Goldston pulled to the side and tipped his hat.

They crested the hill. An open stretch bore left under a brushy roadcut. There, facing them, its right front wheel off and a jack under the frame, sat Ivy Methvin's jalopy truck.

Clyde slowed.

Bonnie said, "Looks like the old man's got tire trouble," and took a bite of her sandwich.

Clyde shifted the rifle from between his knees so that it rested against his left thigh and leaned forward to get a better look. The fingers of his right hand brushed the 45 beside him. Sunlight streamed in just over the treetops. He pushed in the clutch and downshifted and saw his mistake an instant too late.

A month after Bonnie and Clyde met, he was arrested and shortly convicted of seven counts of auto theft and burglary. Because Clyde had effected a brief escape from the Waco Jail, an enraged Judge Richard Munroe slapped a fourteen year sentence on him and assigned him to Eastham, one of the worst prisons in the nation at the time, according to a special report by The Osborne Association that singled it out for its "exceedingly black picture of harsh and brutal treatment."

Clyde arrived at Eastham prison farm, thirteen thousand acres of corn and cotton nestled into a swampy Trinity oxbow in east Texas, on April 21, 1930, a day after the leader of the Nazi Party's forty first birthday and a month after his own twentieth. Records state that he was five feet five and a half inches tall and weighed 127 pounds. He gave a date of birth that was falsified by two years, he claimed his middle name was Champion when it was Chestnut, and he listed Bonnie Parker as his wife, though she was no such thing. He became prisoner number 63527.

Young, small, and polite of manner, Clyde found himself suddenly among murderers, rapists, armed robbers—the state's most hardened criminals, including lifers with no hope of again seeing the outside. Early on, he befriended an inmate close in age named Ralph Fults with whom he was assigned to a gang chopping trees for the woodpile. The youths were given tools and monitored by the guards. They worked alongside the Trinity's spreading waterway, the same river that, two hundred miles north divided Dallas into east and west.

Over snoring saws, the pair sealed their friendship with whispered admiration for western outlaws and with murmurings against the prison's injustices. Years later, in his memoirs, Ralph Fults recalled that Clyde at times would look off into the distance, frozen in what seemed to be a reverie. Jaw set, hands quivering, eyes darkening, Clyde would begin to hiss and sputter, the sounds, Fults figured, simply his lungs leaking out into the muggy air, his body carrying on its work in his mind's absence. But inside the staticky patches, Fults began to catch phrases—"Every time one passes . . . yellow cowards . . . murder these murderers . . . turn the place loose . . ."—and, recognizing them, eventually, for the fantasies they were, Fults indulged their maker.

Bonnie climbed out of bed and stumbled into the front room, where she slipped in and out of sleep until noon, draped over the furniture in various states. A girlfriend called, and they arranged to meet downtown. She dressed and fixed her hair with a handful of hairpins and put on a felt hat, then left her mother a note.

The streetlamps were soft detonations of yellow. She paused outside a restaurant along Murphy Street and looked in at the uppity mugs of a gray haired couple, boldly watching them as a cigaret diminished between her fingers. A newspaper turned in the wind and flew in hitches down the sidewalk. A knot bobbed up in her throat and she swallowed. She'd always wanted only one man who'd be everything to her. With Clyde she could be freely honest. He reveled in her quirks and encouraged her vices. They bore a common spirit that shirked the rich man with his laws and banks and straight edged buildings. But now she was on the other side of all that. He was gone away, and she'd stopped answering his letters.

She walked on through the city blocks aglow with lights, past spots where she and Clyde had strolled hand in hand. She tried but couldn't recall his touch. She passed a shuttered cafe where they'd shared a piece of squash pie, disbelieving her own memory of having slipped him a pistol while he was in the Waco jail, of secreting the piece of iron between her breasts. She could feel, in memory, the cold weight of it against her sternum where she had cinched it with a belt. She rubbed the spot as she walked.

By the time she reached the meeting point, her girlfriend was nowhere in sight. She couldn't recall where all she'd just been, and though she couldn't have said why, she stood there waiting for a very long time.

Just past noon on January 21, 1932, a dark cloud ten thousand feet tall hove into view outside Amarillo. No one had ever seen such an incredible sight. It sprouted an anvil top and where sunlight penetrated its lighter edge, it glowed a fantastical green. Its waist rippled, its sides bristled like fur. A worker for the Weather Bureau described it as "most spectacular" in his log. It wasn't a rain cloud or a tornado and appeared not to carry any moisture at all, not even ice, for those who were closest to its edge felt only pellets of dust stinging their skin.

Shopkeepers left their businesses and stared from street corners. Motorists pulled over, agape. "Like the pillar of smoke given to the Israelites," one woman said.

For several minutes, it lingered on the town's edge as if weighing its options. When it started north, it picked up speed and grew until it was eight miles wide. Ducks and geese tried to outrun it, but their flocks disintegrated and disappeared behind its forward edge. To farmers and ranchers on the Texas panhandle, it appeared like an outsized prophecy, an enormous gray tumbleweed riding a tarblack wind. People banged cellar doors behind them or squeezed under houses. The vortex of currents churned the plowed fields into a cold boil. It lifted chunks of humus the size of housecats and hurled them into the air. A mother caught too far from her farmhouse outside of Dumas tented a wet sheet over her three children and crawled under it with them, and they kneeled and prayed as the storm battered their sides.

Dust, in a wicked marriage with wind, fastened to anything with a hint of moisture: eyeballs, nostrils, mouths. It caked earholes, crusted teeth, weighted beards and mustaches, cinched to scalps and skin. Mexican railroad workers in Dalhart took the storm for the apocalypse and fought their way to the town's Catholic church, where they found a priest and insisted on receiving absolution. Headlights glowed bluish green. Radios and ignitions shorted. A man in Clayton, New Mexico, brushed the elbow of his wife and a bolt of static electricity threw them both to the floor.

The storm stretched doom over everything, as if a piece of outer darkness had torn free from a corner of space and fallen like a shadow over the earth. Those caught inside felt driven toward a reckoning with the unknown. A man caged by the storm confronted the essential alienation of being, made worse by the surprising silence locked within its swirling embrace: the dust particles muffled all sound, even, incredibly, the wind's roar. Where there had been the rustle of dry hay, the hum of a motor, the clap of a loose fence board, now there was only the pure absence of sound.

And on that same day as the first black duster, on the Eastham prison farm, Clyde Barrow—who for more than a year had suffered indignities no one should have to know and who could see nothing of the Amarillo cloud—took off his left shoe and placed his bare foot atop a wood block and nodded to a man in a white prison suit who was wielding an axe. Clyde listened to the whistle of its descent and the wet chunk it made, then watched his two largest toes on that foot somersault through the air like a pair of dominoes and land in the dust.

Tyman Akin had a gentle, pudgy face and skittering eyes. He'd been courting Bonnie for months, and, given his regular work as a deliveryman, was a suitor of whom Emma Parker approved. The pair sat in Emma's front room with the sounds of Emma bustling in the kitchen encouraging their conversation.

Tyman touched a hanky folded into a palm sized square to his upper lip. Bonnie was recalling childhood mischief enacted with cousins on a visit to Oklahoma, reporting that one night they snuck out of the house and commandeered the mine manager's truck. They slipped it into neutral and rolled it down a hill, riding in the bed and howling into the night wind and waking the whole town. She said, "We left the truck intact and parked in front of the Baptist church, lest you think poorly of me for sporting that way."

"It strikes me as a devilish prank," Tyman teased.

She started to tell of another shenanigan with the selfsame cousins, but a knock at the door interrupted. When she opened it, she shrieked, said "Darling!" then flung her arms around the visitor's neck.

"How's my baby been?" the man said.

Emma went ash gray when, peeping from the kitchen, she found her daughter liplocked to Clyde Barrow. She squeezed the blood from her hands and glanced at Tyman, where he sat on the couch turning red. When Clyde saw Mrs. Parker, he said hello and shifted his hand from Bonnie's backside to his crutch handle.

Bonnie glowed, electric and curious. "Why didn't you call? How long have you been free? Why are you stumping around on these thingamajigs?" She had no patience for answers but caressed and pulled him inside. When she turned around, Emma's severe nod toward Tyman inspired her to offer a clumsy introduction.

Tyman gathered himself to stand, but Clyde held up a cautionary wave. "Don't get up, you'll just make me feel crippled."

The two men stationed at either end of the couch as Clyde gave the details of his release, including his poorly timed adventure with the axe, which turned out to be unnecessary since Governor Ross Sterling, in response to Cumie's repeated appeals for her son's release, signed Clyde's pardon papers without knowledge of the injury.

"It's all right, though," Clyde said. "My other eight toes is working better than ever. I guess they're scared of the same treatment."

Emma excused herself with a flustered smile. Bonnie had alighted on the couch arm closest to Clyde, her hands flitting over his shoulder and collar and arm like a pair of hummingbirds charmed by a fresh blossom. She complimented him on his blue silk shirt. The color of desire, she said.

"It seems like there hasn't been a blue sky around here for months," Tyman said, adding that his mother had an inch of pumice dust on her floors and had taken to tacking paraffin soaked sheets around the windows and flapping the air with a wet towel.

Clyde shook his head and addressed Bonnie as if Tyman were a wall decoration. "You ought to see the station these days, Bon. Nehis go out the front for a nickel, and pap's pick me up goes out the back for a dime."

Tyman swiped his skull and said to the room at large, "I was thinking of going to Sugie's this Saturday."

"That old place?" Bonnie said, her voice stripped of propriety but holding no meanness. "Their beer tastes like warm spit."

As cheerily as he could, Tyman said, "I'd better get on," and took his leave.

Bonnie climbed into Clyde's lap before the door shut. They kissed. And kissed again and lingered over each other. Clyde brushed her cheek with his thumb. "And I was sure you wouldn't have me back."

"You must be up the pole to think such a thing. You turn my light on like no one else, Clyde Barrow."

Emma looked in. "Where did Mr. Akin go?"

"He had to leave," Bonnie said.

Emma clutched the doorjamb, supervisory and stern. She began folding and refolding a thin cotton towel in the air until Clyde grew uncomfortable and scooted Bonnie to his knee. Emma stepped forward and delivered the speech she'd just prepared. "Listen, Clyde, if you want to go with Bonnie, that's all right with me. But you ought to get a job first and prove that everything is going to be all right."

"Shucks, Mrs. Parker," Clyde said. "Even if I did get a regular job, no decent girl would go with me, would they, honey?"

Bonnie giggled and pinched his earlobe, thrilled by the strange compliment.

"Now don't talk that way," Emma said. "Many a good boy has gotten in trouble and gone to the pen. There's no reason why you can't make good and go straight."

"Nobody would give me a job in this town."

Emma withdrew a little. "You don't know that for certain."

"My sister Nell's been talking with friends she has in Massachusetts."

"Way up there?" Bonnie said.

Emma tucked the towel under her arm and shrugged, the picture of motherly indulgence. "Maybe you'd like it somewhere new. And surely that's far enough that the law wouldn't be knowing every time you stuck your head out of the door. Things would work out. Bonnie will still be here."

When Emma returned to the kitchen, Clyde said, "I bet your mama'd buy my train ticket if I asked."

"Shush."

Clyde nodded at Tyman's lingering presence. "How many more like him have you got? I figure there's bound to be a passel."

"You've vanquished your only rival." She laid a hand on his crutches. "Good thing you brought your swords. You're like a wounded soldier home from the war."

"And you my patient bride."

"You ought to be throwing me over for not having written you more."

"For all you know, we might've both been old and gray by the time I got out. I don't hold nothing against you." He regarded a wallprint of Jesus doling bread to a mob of children. "But I weren't going to stay there the rest of my life, I promise you that."

Bonnie made to tousle his hair but thought better and cupped the back of his neck. "You're always on the fast end of the chase."

"I guess I have to be, baby."

She caressed his jaw, then turned to him. "Have you been lonesome for me?"

It was the youthful, carefree Clyde who answered with a smile that creased his cheeks. "Only as lonesome as a preacher on payday."

Clyde did try briefly to go straight, but Dallas at the time was so job starved and its breadlines so clogged that the city leaders called for all the negro unemployed to evacuate and move to the country where, they were assured, farmers had stores of grain housed and ready for them. Clyde wheedled a job from a former employer, but the police found him in his first week and began picking him up on suspicion until he was fired. The pattern repeated through three positions. Then, on Nell's insistence and industry, he caught the train to Framingham, Massachusetts, and for two weeks, as Jack Stuwart, staggered behind a wheelbarrow filled with sloshing concrete before the lack of family and friends and the strangeness of the East and the longing for Bonnie compelled him back to Dallas and Nell's waiting wrath. What he told her was, "Nothing means a damn to me but all of you. If I have to be away from yall, I might as well be dead."

He tried one last job, though, as a rehire at United Glass and Mirror, then on March 15, after being fired yet again for missing work while being interrogated by the Dallas police as a suspect in a crime he didn't commit, waving the three dollars in his hand he'd earned that week, what Clyde said to Cumie as he stormed in the front room was, "Mama, I aint going back to work."

Outside of town he mechanicks on the carburetor, bending the lid spring just so.

Trees and fence posts flicker past. A tan fog billows behind.

How is it he's so comfortable. Says calmly over the roar, We're now traveling at one hundred miles per hour.

Life feels close, her mother's kitchen table far. She braces the heels of her hands against the dash, the door. Her heart kicks. Maybe it's mischief, sheer ignorance, the ever distance of death.

Blind hills. Deadman curves. One blown tire at this speed. Shrieking engine, squalling shocks, disintegrating frame: calls to worship.

A trace of a smile bends the impassive mountain of his mouth. The world so far has asked so little. Now it wants everything.

She reaches into the blur.

Can't it go any faster, she yells.

He smirks and pulls down the spark lever.

It was in the spring of 1932 that Clyde fell easily back into criminal life and drew Bonnie with him. By early April, Clyde and the newly released Ralph Fults were discussing a raid on Eastham from the outside that would free as many inmates as possible. Along the way they partnered with Ray Hamilton, another West Dallas upstart, on a bank job in Lawrence, Kansas, and scored $33,000, an astounding sum at the time, but blew most of it on a swindle when they purchased a bum arsenal from a pawnshop in Illinois. The pistols and tommy guns jammed or failed to fire, and the bulletproof vests proved unworthy of their name.

Still, Ralph Fults and Clyde pressed on and formed, from a menagerie of ex cons, a group that called itself the Lake Dallas Gang. They organized a pair of bank jobs and began scouting ways to procure high caliber weaponry. As well, they would need to contact someone on the inside. A lifer name Aubrey Scalley, one of the Camp Two building tenders, had once done Clyde a favor. On April 17, Bonnie was sent to Eastham to pay Scalley a visit.

She strolled into the administrative office wearing a grass green felt hat with a silver buckle, a matching dress with butterfly sleeves, and high heels with peep toes. Having prearranged the meeting on the fiction that Scalley was her cousin, she gained quick admission, then swaggered across the front room, drawing the attention of every guard and inmate in sight.

A tender escorted her down a hallway that smelled powerfully of bleach to a room where gray cracks webbed the otherwise white walls. A thin window admitted a fallen column of sunlight just outside of which sat a giant man in a white tee shirt and white trousers. He was shaved, and his hair had been carefully oiled and combed front to back. A mushroom nose and underbite made him look slow of mind. "Aint you the prettiest thing I've seen in a month of Sundays."

Bonnie smiled and sat, and at Scalley's nod, the other tender shut the door, then Scalley unrolled a pack of cigarets from his shirt sleeve and tamped it against his palm. He pushed one up from the packet bottom and pulled it out with his lips. A wheel lighter appeared from somewhere on his person. When he sparked it, the wick cover uncapped a yellow flame. He watched her as he breathed life into his cigaret, and though she remained as poised as a stage actress, he didn't fail to notice one of her knees pistoning like the needle on a sewing machine.

He shucked loose the stub of another cigaret and held it out. As she took it and the offered light, she glanced at the door's tiny window.

"Don't worry none about them," he said. "They're my underlings. They do as I say. Word is you might be carrying more than a weather report."

Bonnie explained that her companions were sequestered in the woods a mile off. Then she detailed the composition of the Lake Dallas Gang and the pending raid. "Butch," she said—by which she meant Clyde—"plans to free as many cons as possible." She spoke fast and in the silence that followed seemed unsure whether the man had caught her meaning.

Scalley snapped a trickle of ash onto the floor. "I suppose all the long riders around here will just roll over and play possum. What's he propose to do with the guards crawling all over this place?"

As if reporting something as commonplace as the health of a distant aunt, Bonnie said, "He proposes to shoot every goddamn one of them."

Scalley's laughter, rhonchial and sharp, erupted off the walls. Two rows of snaggled gray teeth sat in his mouth like cave mice. The other tender's face appeared briefly at the window but nothing else. Scalley shook his head, sobered at some thought, then said, "Well, and why shouldn't he."

Bonnie added the plan for the next day: Clyde and Fults would nick a pair of cars up in Tyler, large and speedy enough to pull off a grand escape. When the gang roared up, the guards would be taken by complete surprise. Eastham was so remote, no one would suspect an attack from outside.

"I watched him kill a man once. He ever tell you that story?" Bonnie shook her head and Scalley fell to coughing. "Well, as long as we're dreaming, tell your

Butch we'll want some roscoes of our own. We don't expect to be rolling away from here with only our limp dicks swinging between our knees."

A light ignited in Bonnie's eyes. "Is that how you would speak to a lady, Mr. Aubrey Scalley?"

"No, but it's how I like to speak to you."

Bonnie stood and smoothed her dress. She flipped a lock of hair off her forehead and squelched the comment rising in her mind—about the man's mother—and instead stepped toward him into the sunlight column, where she became a blinding blade of green. She dropped the cigaret to the floor and snuffed it with a toetip. "The other four are in Celina procuring an arsenal as we speak."

Scalley smiled lewdly with his gray teeth and called her heaven's loveliest angel and took her hand.

She matched his sugary tone precisely as she said, "It's a delight to deliver swell tidings."

Scalley carved a piece of breakfast from between his teeth with a thumbnail and regarded it and then Bonnie, enshrined before him in morning glory. "Tell your boy that my estimation of him has jumped a few notches after meeting you." He rubbed the back of her hand with his thumb, and she snatched it away.

"I'd take it as high praise if you'll tell him yourself when you're both on the outside later this week." Then she crossed to the door and rapped on it.

"And just when we were getting acquainted," Scalley said. "Tell me before you go, miss, because all the chins are wagging. They say your boy made a pot of dough on a bank job up in Kansas."

She regarded one of the gray cracks rising off the doorframe, then spoke to him over her shoulder. "This dress and these shoes were purchased last week in cash. And I've got half a dozen outfits even spiffier that I just can't wait to wear."

The door opened. She winked and sashayed through.

Scalley's voice chased her down the hallway. "You'll be a darb of the season in each and every one."

The day after Bonnie's visit to Scalley, she and Fults were arrested outside of Kaufman, Texas, after a bungled attempt to burglarize weapons from a hardware store. Only Clyde escaped and made it back home, where he organized a robbery of a general store in Hillsboro with members of the Lake Dallas Gang, his intention that of funding a jailbreak for Fults to prevent his landing back at Eastham (Clyde presumed that Bonnie, with no strikes against her and enjoying the privilege of being a female, would soon be set free).

During the Hillsboro robbery, the store owner, an optician named John Bucher, grabbed a pistol and was shot dead by Ted Rogers, a trigger happy hoodlum who closely resembled Ray Hamilton. When officers later pressed John Bucher's wife to identify potential suspects from a row of photographs they twice laid out on her kitchen counter, she fingered Ray, who hadn't been along, and Clyde, who'd been parked outside, waiting in the getaway car. The authorities incorrectly named Ray and Clyde as the killers, and thereafter, the fates of the two were linked in ways that would never be undone.

For the time being the prison raid was bust. The other cons in the Lake Dallas Gang scattered or stumbled into arrest. Similarly spectered by the electric chair, Ray Hamilton rejoined Clyde. Ray was small and sinewy like Clyde but four years younger. He was a fast talker, kept his wispy blond hair clipped short and neat, and in a handshake only gave a man his fingers. His blue eyes were of the color that people called piercing. Ray was the fourth of six kids deserted by their father, and Old Lady Hamilton kept a frame house across the road from the Barrow filling station. Ray was another West Dallas delinquent who'd caught the attention of the Dallas police early on, having been first arrested at fourteen for stealing a toy wagon. After days of being locked up on charges that were only occasionally accurate, he'd come home exhausted, angry, bruised.

In July, Clyde and Ray rented a house in Wichita Falls, and it's this hiatus that has led to speculation that the two young hoods from West Dallas found a camaraderie early on that reached beyond their link in the public consciousness as killers. Maybe. To the consternation of many a scrutator, sexuality doesn't fossilize. We do know that Bonnie was soon released from jail as Clyde had predicted. She joined Clyde and Ray, writing to her mother that she'd landed cafe work and was living with a girlfriend.

On an August night in Stringtown, Oklahoma, near an open air pavilion, Sheriff Charlie Maxwell confronted two strangers who, sipping whiskey in their car and taking turns dancing with the girls, had been upsetting the young men. When the sheriff placed a boot on the car's running board and spoke of arrest, one of the strangers shot him six times—and though he would, improbably, survive, his deputy, Eugene Moore, who returned fire, was killed outright by a single shot to the head. The strangers fled into the night.

There was a third man with the outsiders named Ross Dyer. He'd been on the dance floor at the time of the shooting and was able to slip away in the confusion and board a bus. But he was picked up later that night and returned to Atoka County, where, under interrogation, he named his accomplices: Clyde Barrow and Ray Hamilton.

The trio of Bonnie, Clyde, and Ray then made for Carlsbad, New Mexico, where Bonnie had an aunt, but an inquisitive sheriff's deputy ruined their plans for cooling off. They kidnapped the deputy, drove him back into Texas, and released him outside of San Antonio. When the man called authorities from a farmhouse, he was surprised to hear that his headless corpse had been found outside of El Paso the night before. The case of mistaken identity had alerted officers across Texas. Roadblocks were set—and one, over the Colorado River in Wharton, nearly netted the desperadoes.

It was after such escapades that Ray opted to quit the arrangement. As close as he and Clyde may have been, the two could never endure together for long. Ray complained about camping, was bored by guns, and grew to believe that the only worthwhile targets were banks, deriding Clyde's preference for smaller jobs.

In early September, then, Bonnie and Clyde drove Ray Hamilton to Bay City, Michigan, where his father lived, and dropped him off. On their return trip, the couple traveled east until they hit the shores of Lake Huron, then veered down country, skirting Lake St. Clair and passing through Henry Ford's Detroit before admiring Lake Erie and heading west. In Chicago, they craned their necks at skyscrapers and strolled through concrete canyons. They stole a series of cars along the way and sponsored their travels by robbing laundries and filling stations. Clyde carried a flathead screwdriver in his pocket and wasn't above jimmying a gumball machine for a handful of pennies and a joke as he spilled them double handed into Bonnie's lap.

It was during this time that the couple joined the ranks of motor gypsies who towed trailers or otherwise made of their autos their abodes. Bonnie and Clyde stayed at cabin camps for two dollars a night and purchased sandwiches and coffee from stores filled with tacky souvenirs. Along back roads in Kansas and Missouri, they saw lilac dawns and empty fields and the lonely lights of nowhere towns. They stopped and slept at farmhouses, and, in return for hospitality, they left behind a dollar bill or a present in the form of a loaf of bread or a block of cheese. They sent home unsigned postcards, listing the sights they'd seen and their doings. In Kansas City, they had their nails done. They listened to music and danced. Bonnie got a permanent from a lady who gasped at her wolflike eyes and gave her a discount because she was so pretty.

Into late autumn the pair lived off paltry takings and kept a low profile. Bonnie more often than not rode pressed against Clyde's shoulder, drawing his warmth and watching the sights slide past. Yellow swaths of tobacco. Brown fields filled with rows of crooked black needles—all that was left of the spindled cotton. Wind ruined farms reclaimed by weeds. He liked to drive with his shucked wingtips askew in the floorboard, and Bonnie did likewise, shedding flats or heels, her choice of footwear dependent on their pursuers' proximity. They drove under mackerel skies and through the plains towns, each with a bank, hotel, cafe, and telephone office. One town ran together with all the others, Childress, Chillicothe, Coldwater, Tucumcari, Walsh, Watonga. They entered a backwoods country threaded with brushy creeks, where they drove past the tree draped knots of Queen Wilhelmina Mountain, Iron Mountain, Shadow Mountain.

In their early days of running, Clyde was often sullen, prison having changed him, while Bonnie was charming and chatty. When they stayed at tourist cabins, they dyed their hair, an hours long, painstaking process. Bonnie fussed over each step and scolded Clyde for trying to unwrap the turbaned towel too soon. They would leave a handful of suits and dresses at a smalltown laundry, then lose themselves in the countryside while they waited, risking capture for the comfort of clean clothes.

Yet they rode most often without destination, tired and hungry, and when Clyde could go no farther, he turned down a deer trail or found a dry creekbed or an abandoned orchard, and there they shut themselves inside the car or spread the seat cushions on the ground and slept with mosquitoes furring their skin. They squatted behind bushes and wiped themselves with leaves. They bathed in icy creeks with a sliver of soap. They sweated during the day and froze at night. They ate their meals cold: canned stew, dry crackers, cheese sandwiches, beans in tomato paste. If they did risk a campfire, it was to boil weenies in a lard can or to fry a flitch of bacon.

When they stayed with farmers, they ate what was offered. Come morning, the barefoot children would clamber onto the running boards and demand a ride. Clyde would dutifully fire up the motor and swing the stolen car around the yard and pick up speed and burst through dust curtains as his passengers' rodeo whoops wiped the dullness of sleep from his face and replaced it with a bent grin.

W. D. Jones, The 1968 *Playboy* Interview : First of Six Fragments

I had got with Clyde and Bonnie one night in Dallas. Me and L. C., that's Clyde's younger brother, was driving home from a dance in his daddy's old truck. This was on Christmas Eve 1932. Here come Bonnie and Clyde. They honked their car horn and we pulled over. I stayed in the truck. L. C. got out and went back to see what they wanted.

Then he hollered at me. "Hey, come on back. Clyde wants to talk to you."

Clyde was wanted then for murder and kidnapping, but I had knowed him all my life.

He told me, "We're here to see mama and Marie." (That's Clyde's younger sister.) "You stay with us while L. C. gets them."

I was sixteen years old and Clyde was only six years older, but he always called me "boy."

After the visiting was over, Clyde said him and Bonnie had been driving a long ways and was tired. He wanted me to go with them so I could keep watch while they got some rest. I went. I know now it was a fool thing to do, but then it seemed sort of big to be out with two famous outlaws. I reckoned Clyde took me along because he had knowed me before and figured he could count on me.

It must have been two o'clock Christmas morning when we checked into a tourist court at Temple. They slept on the bed. I had a pallet on the floor.

Next morning, we went into town and stopped around the corner from a grocery store. Clyde handed me an old .41 caliber and told me, "Take this, boy, and stand watch while I get us some spending money."

I stood outside the store while Clyde went in. Bonnie was waiting in the car around the corner. After he got the money, we walked away toward Bonnie. Before we got halfway back to the car, Clyde stopped along a Model A roadster that had the keys in it. I don't know if he'd seen something over his shoulder that spooked him or what. But he told me, "Get in that car, boy, and start it."

I jumped to it. But it was a cold day, and the car wouldn't start. Clyde got impatient. He told me to slip over and he'd do it. I scooted over.

About then an old man and an old woman run over to the roadster and began yelling, "That's my boy's car! Get out!"

Then another woman run up and began making a big fuss. All the time, Clyde was trying to get it started. He told them to stand back and they wouldn't get hurt. Then the guy who owned it run up.

Clyde pointed his pistol and yelled, "Get back, man, or I'll kill you!"

That man was Doyle Johnson, I learned later. He came on up to the car and reached through the roadster's isinglass window curtains and got Clyde by the throat and tried to choke him.

Clyde hollered. "Stop, man, or I'll kill you."

Johnson didn't move, and Clyde done what he had threatened. About then he got the car started, and we whipped around the corner to where Bonnie was waiting. We piled into her car and lit a shuck out of town.

It all seemed pointless then as to why Clyde wanted that car. I've thought about it since, and I figure he must have wanted the laws to think we was in Johnson's car. Of course, he didn't have no way of knowing he was gonna have to kill Johnson.

We headed out of town. He was pushing that Ford for all it was worth toward Waco. "What you gonna do, honey?" Bonnie asked Clyde. "You can't go back to Dallas now. That man's shot and probably dead." He was, too, we found out later.

"Hell, I know that. He can't go back either," Clyde said, nodding at me. "You know that, don't you, boy? You got murder on you, just like me. You can't go home."

They was supposed to take me home to Dallas that Christmas Day. He had promised that, but I couldn't go home after Doyle Johnson got killed. I was an outlaw, too, now, so I stayed with them. The robbing and the killing never stopped, and neither did we.

For me, that's how it all started.

Who were Bonnie and Clyde? They were children
of the wilderness whose wilderness had been razed.
—Nelson Algren

Work at Eastham, whether on a cotton line or a wood chopping detail, meant agony from sunup to sundown. Work weeks were six days long when they weren't seven, which is to say, when it wasn't harvest. Inmates joked about the eight hour workdays: eight in the morning, eight in the evening. At daybreak, each prisoner received a breakfast pittance—often stale bread and rancid bacon—then lined up to run single file to the fields or woods. In case a prisoner slowed, the guards carried pitchforks.

Each work squad was surrounded by two rings of guards, the inner with long tom shotguns, and the outer horse mounted highriders with winchester 30 30s. Some prisoners chose death by shotgun. Others injected kerosene or filthy water into their muscles to trigger infections or drank liquefied shoe polish in the hopes of landing in the infirmary.

Inmates who made trouble were stripped nude, cuffed, and put into a box called The Shitter, a corrugated tin structure set in full sun and made to such narrow dimensions that its occupant was unable to sit. Leaning also was impossible since solar glare heated the walls to searing. No food or drink was given. The occupant's mouth would go oven dry, his legs would turn to melted rubber, and his mind to mush. Those kept inside too long would suffocate on their own tongues.

Yet Eastham's most hated punishment was the Pink Master, a leather strap as long as a man's leg attached to a wooden handle and greased with linseed oil. The inmate selected for special treatment would be stripped and held facedown by fellow prisoners as the guards took giddy turns lashing him across the back, buttocks, and legs. The man would inevitably scream and spill his bowels, but the session only stopped after he blacked out from pain. The bat received its name for this reason: those who restrained the man would leave the beating with their white uniforms tinted pink.

3

WELLINGTON

May 23rd

Until that truck came
along in the wrong lane,
they lived on gravy and grits,
that is to say, on luck and wits,

But reaching toward
all those stolen Fords
was the hand of Death,
its fingers stretched,

tapping at the glass
as if to ask
a question about burdens
and how justice needs serving.

What justice, you might say,
is served by the spray
of bullets from head to toe?
Only this: we all must go.

March 26th, 1933

Within seventy two hours of Buck Barrow's release from the Texas state penitentiary in Huntsville on March 22, 1933, the Reichstag voted to abolish democracy in favor of the dictatorship of Adolph Hitler; the freshly inaugurated President Roosevelt signed into law a bill legalizing the manufacture and sale of three two beer; and Clyde Barrow, despite being sought for multiple murders, tracked down his older brother to where he was spending the night with his wife at her stepfather's farmhouse twenty miles south of Dallas.

The sedan rolled in under night's canvas, its brush of light sweeping across the slatted ribs of Holsteins. One wobbled to its feet, dull pupils aglow, to acknowledge the intruder. The night was cold, and as the three occupants clambered from the sedan, they translated scents of cow plop and hay and earth damp into vapor balloons. Bonnie pulled from a flask and took in the night sky with its shock points of light.

"Damn it smells good out here," she said.

The man who answered the door was wearing a threadbare robe over flannel bottoms and a tee shirt gray from sweat. He didn't recognize the visitors, who were asking for Buck Barrow, though the short, dapper one in front resembled a law student or a young doctor. Soon enough, their voices drew Buck himself downstairs.

Though seven years older than Clyde, Buck was an inch shorter and twenty pounds lighter. Prison had hardly touched him. He clapped Clyde on the back and proclaimed, "Well, I'll be. Smelling of jittersauce and gasoline, just like I left you." He received a cheek kiss from Bonnie and pumped W. D.'s hand, then he cracked a joke about midnight surprises and escorted them upstairs where, under slant ceilings, they found a tiny bedroom that smelled of camphor.

Blanche was sitting up in the bed under a pile of quilts, rubbing her eyes and shushing a little white dog in the bed with her.

Bonnie's voice snagged on a sob as she threw her arms around Blanche. "Haven't seen you in a coon's age."

The dog held its forepaws in the air and wagged its bushy tail.

"They look like two dolls, don't they?" Buck said.

"We *are* two dolls," Blanche said, "in case you didn't know." She peeled back the quilts and patted the bed, and Bonnie crawled under, complaining about not having been to the beauty shop in ages.

"Turn that down," Clyde said, pointing to a coal oil lamp burning on a side table.

W. D. spun the wick until its light cast a tiny dome, then he moved to the window and kept lookout.

Clyde leaned the shotgun he was harboring against the wall, and the group exchanged the news. Clyde joked about robbing laundries for sacks of nickels to use as gas money. At first, he nodded at Buck's prison report, but when it contained no ire of injustice—held as Buck was, on light duty inside the main prison—Clyde's eyes hooded and he only half listened and eventually began mumbling his own abstract list of wrongs. At one point he suggested that Buck and Blanche might help him in a plan he was forming.

Blanche had heard something of this sort of talk before from Clyde on visits during his incarceration, but never had he hinted at involving others in the family. Her voice hissed out. "As if it's not bad enough, you bringing your guns into my stepfather's house. Your brother's not been out three days. He's just come off fourteen months in the pen. We're trying to set up a straight life, buy a house in Dallas and settle down, and here you want to send him right back."

Clyde backtracked, reasoned, and explained that she and Buck wouldn't have to do anything illegal, merely pass notes to one of the inmates.

W. D. poured water from a tin pitcher into a jar. He kept his gaze fixed on the window as he drank, and the others watched him watch that dark rectangle.

Blanche crossed her arms in a huff. "I just don't see any percentage in it, that's all." The dog tasted her elbow with its tongue, then leaned against the pillow as if it was aware some important point had been settled.

When the men grew cold, they went down and sat in the car. Clyde slid the heat register open and turned over the engine. Buck's search discovered a quart jar wrapped in newspaper on the floorboard. In between sips, he fiddled with the bipod mounted on the dash and meant for a rifle's muzzle. Clyde rehearsed the story of trolling the streets of Marshall, Texas, when he saw a man pull up to the curb in the sedan and hurry into a house carrying a bottle of milk, having left the car running. "There couldn't have been a more open invitation," Clyde said, but the story was meant only to pass the time and there was no need to listen closely.

There were no passing cars, just the darkling view of the farmhouse. The heat and the engine's purr whiled them toward sleep. Outside, the night pooled around the tires and crept up the fenders. The next Clyde knew, he jerked awake. He sat there with blood speeding through his veins, and it was in that hypnopompic state that he stirred Buck and gave form to a new idea. He reported an "endless" store of money from a recent take in Ash Grove, Missouri, and animated in Buck's mind how weary Bonnie was from not seeing her mother and how the five of them ought to hole up somewhere for a week or two. Joplin, maybe, where the laws looked the other way and the bootleggers did as they pleased. They could take an apartment. The women might prettify the place with five and dime trinkets while all of them luxuriated for a time. Afterward, Clyde said, Buck and Blanche could take the decorations with them for their first home.

Upstairs, Bonnie hummed a radio tune. She kissed Blanche's neck. "Stay strong on yall's freedom. You've waited so long for your Buck to be free."

Blanche cupped Bonnie's jaw, then set her cheek against the girl's head. "Darling, you're so tired. At least close your eyes and pretend to sleep."

"I'd rather talk with you. It's been so long since we've seen each other."

And they did talk, on through the night, of Bonnie's longing for a real bed and of Blanche's love of photography. She showed Bonnie some snapshots and offered to let her borrow her box camera. They kept each other awake until the first sliver of blue split earth from the sky, and Buck and Clyde returned with the new plan.

April 27th, 1933

Clyde pistol whipped the man. Watched his legs sprawl like a stunned calf's as he slumped against the turtleback.

"What's your name?"

It took the man a few seconds to stammer out, "Dillard Darby."

Clyde nuzzled his face next to Dillard Darby's ear, where a blood line was zipping past a dried speck of shaving cream, then he laced his fingers through Darby's hair and yanked back. He set the barrel mouth against the man's temple, whispered, "My plans don't include you," and snicked back the 45's hammer.

Darby's eyes strayed.

"You going to finish the job or not?" Buck said, having come up from behind.

When the hammer snapped on a dead cap, Clyde said, "I guess that one weren't meant for you," and Darby never did discover if Clyde had planted the dead cap or if he was saved by providence or blind fortune.

The Joplin reunion had gone south when a group of officers acting on neighborhood complaints, but suspecting only lightly armed bootleggers, converged on the Barrows at their rented garage apartment. While Bonnie spiderwebbed window glass with a pistol from the second story, Clyde and W. D. fired on the lawmen from the relative safety of the garage below. They killed Constable Wes Harryman and Detective Harry McGinnis. W. D. was shot in the side. The group then roared off, leaving Snowball, Blanche's little white dog, trotting behind in road dust. Buck didn't fire a shot, but he and Blanche were now members of the deadly Barrow gang, such as it was.

Buck said, "Try another one," then hacked up a wad of gleim and spat it arcing into the weeds.

Clyde told Darby, "Get in the car, we're taking you with us," then turned to Darby's companion and said, "You, too, lady."

When Sophia Stone gaped blankly, Clyde said, "Shiiit," and beckoned to Bonnie, who jumped out with a 45 in hand. She yanked Sophia Stone by the arm, but the woman was welded to her seat. An umbrella of dust rose over an approaching car in the distance. Miss Stone seemed not to notice the urgency around her. Bonnie sighed, said, "Damn you," and bashed her in the head with the pistol, but the blow pillowed into the woman's bun. Bonnie then pointed the 45 at her. "You think I aint got the melt to use this?"

"Oh, god, please don't shoot me."

"Then put some skedaddle in that ass."

The pair of hostages were forced into the Ford's backseat with Buck and Blanche. Miss Stone funked at the body reek and held a hand over her mouth. Buck shook his head and muttered threats, then sprawled his legs. The hostages huddled against the door. Bonnie settled into the passenger seat, tugging her dress hem. After the approaching car passed, Clyde began hunting for W. D., whom he called "Deacon" in front of the strangers and who was driving somewhere in Darby's stolen car. He stopped at times and sounded a police siren and finally located tire tracks on a country lane and a crossrutted pullout where someone had doubled back, but the trail played out.

When asked, Sophia Stone gave her name. She was wearing a red cotton dress trimmed in white that contrasted nicely with her dark hair. Her eyes were scoured and raw, and she twisted a kerchief in her hands while Darby pressed the one she gave him to the back of his head. When the identity of their captors dawned on her, she gasped, then began weeping and pleading for her life.

Buck shoved his face in hers, eyes agog. "I got an idea," he said. "Let's us stop the car, tie them up, and blow their brains out."

Miss Stone swooned. Though the hostages were merely neighbors (the newspapers would wrongly label them an engaged couple), Darby held Miss Stone like a lover, one arm across her shoulders, the other massaging her arms and hands back to life as he swore that if they'd had any idea, they wouldn't have given chase when the gang stole his car.

Clyde cursed them as meddlers with no trace of horse sense, but when Darby began to describe the general regard for the Barrow name, claiming that a single officer would no more consider taking them on than he would the German army, Clyde's anger receded somewhat. Buck huffed and tipped up his flask, then sat back as the ride fell into a glum monotony awaiting some unknown end.

With the sun on the horizon, Clyde turned onto a paved road. Bonnie's mood brightened. She complimented Miss Stone on her dress and inquired about her line of work.

"I'm a home demonstration agent for Lincoln Parish," she said, but her voice was so thin and far away that it sounded as if that life had already passed into the realm of remote memory.

Bonnie tucked her bare feet under her and rummaged for a cigaret. "I'm so hungry I could eat anything that don't eat me first." She ashed into an empty shoe, said, "Mexican ashtray," then settled in and listened to Sophia Stone sob. Finally, she said, "Oh, hush," and asked whether she'd cooked anything that day.

"Yes, mam. I was at the school, giving a cooking lesson."

"What was it?"

"Lima bean casserole."

"With cornbread?"

"No mam, but I might have. Hotwater cornbread in muffin tins only takes twenty minutes."

"Mama always called that sort of thing worthless for how dry it turns out."

"Do you take butter on yours?"

"Hell, you can't put enough butter on my hoecake."

Over the next half hour, Miss Stone, pressed by Bonnie, gave her actual menu—chicken and dumplings, oysters Louisiana, turnip greens, spoon bread, fried okra, yam pone, sweet potato souffle, roasting ears (Bonnie: "I could eat a whole peck right this minute"), honey cakes, hot banana pudding, Shreveport pie, apple pandowdy—before being goaded by Bonnie's eager nods and the occasional moan into canvassing dishes she'd only heard of.

Somehow Miss Stone became convinced that her life would end once she exhausted her menu, so she resorted to imagination. But as her specialty dishes edged away from the unusual into the fabulous— skunk fritters, dandelion pudding, rabbit hair soup— her strategy inspired some strange looks. At Bonnie's "eww" when she listed butterfried rattlesnake brains, Miss Stone faltered and started begging to be dropped off in Texarkana, where she had an uncle. When Buck explained that he was going to shoot her where she sat if she uttered another word, she fell catatonic, failing every few minutes to stifle a whimper.

The country flashed by, a brownscape scarred now and then by green. Bonnie moved on to Mr. Darby and discovered him to be an undertaker at the McClure Funeral Home. At this she clapped her hands and doubled over with laughter, the stray hairs that'd escaped her tam brushing the dash. She looked out as if through wet goggles, her eyes were so big.

"You like to make me shit myself," she said, though none of the others seemed to register the joke. When she gathered enough air to speak, she said, "Promise to embalm us when we get ours, Mr. Darby. Say that you'll fix us up real nice, oh please, say that you will."

Darby scrunched his brows.

A sudden sobriety infected Bonnie. She looked him in the eye and in a voice rife with Hollywood melodrama said, "Tell the truth, *Mis tuh Dah by,* you'd embalm us this instant if you could, would you not?"

Darby jammed his eyeglasses up his nose slope and said, "I hope and pray that you all will live long and full lives."

At that, Bonnie's eyes disappeared inside the lines on her face as she gave herself over to waves of happy release, laughing with the forgetfulness of a monk. The others shrugged and sent away their gazes—toward a farmhouse with the curtains drawn for a death, empty fields, an overturned chuck wagon, distant cumulus.

After some time, Bonnie rested, empty, her jaw cupped in her palm and her head leaned against the glass, a child dreaming of a world not so different from hers in which the sun kept motherly watch over everything below, the slow growing trees and the birds singing and the forest creatures moving and the fish slipping in formation through silver streams. Before long, she was asleep.

Darby and Stone were released outside of Waldo, Arkansas. Clyde fluttered a five dollar bill from the window. In the days and years to come, the pair told and retold their tale to anyone who cared to ask.

After that, Clyde moseyed the gang east, stopping frequently, taking regular meals, and sleeping in real beds in tourist cabins. They acquired some Mexican weed, and Bonnie held a bud in her palm for Blanche to sniff.

"My, it's skunky, isn't it?"

Buck winked at Clyde. "They say it will destroy your moral character."

"Don't worry," Bonnie shot back. "He hasn't got one of those."

They stole a car for Buck and Blanche, who followed behind. They posed for snapshots embracing, kissing, holding each other at gunpoint. All this was in the late spring of 1933, before grudges had ruined the group's joie de vivre. In time they would return to Dallas and W. D. would rejoin them, but for now it was just the two couples.

At Mobile, they cleaned the cars, rearranged the luggage, and concealed the guns under tightly tucked blankets. Bonnie purchased a newspaper that she folded into manageable portions, and as they crossed into Florida under a wide open sky, she said, "Would you listen to this. It says here they're introducing a tree from Australia into the Everglades. *For three years, real estate developers have used a squadron of flivver planes to sow seeds of the melaleuca tree over a vast territory. The melaleuca takes water at an enormous rate and will dry out an acre of swamp in a short time. Though homely, the tree is fitted well to the harsh life of the swamp and exhibits a singular trait in the face of death. When chopped, poisoned, frozen, or burned, it releases twenty million seeds to the wind and resows itself in every direction imaginable.*"

Clyde was gazing out the window as if seeing there not the flash of pine and scrub, but rolling acres clumped with cypress and cattails and, above it all, a field of white trunked trees looming like towers fashioned from bone.

"That there's one helluva tree," Clyde said.

At Tallahassee, the four stopped at a roadhouse to enjoy beer and wine, newly on menus everywhere, and a dinner of fried catfish and green beans cooked with bacon. When the first round of drinks arrived, Bonnie raised her glass, said, "Mud in your eye," and officially initiated the vacation. And after crossing Florida's neck and reaching the coast, they followed it north into Georgia, where they took a two lane bridge to Amelia Island and the town of Fernandina Beach.

They'd planned to go on to Jacksonville, but the surf and sun were such a welcome respite that they stayed for days, bathing in the ocean and lounging on towels at the water's edge. Clyde retrieved a tin coffeepot from the car and constructed crenellated towers and palace complexes with cathedrals and great halls that he protected with enormous bastions. Boys in bathing suits gaped at the sandworks and pleaded to help. He recruited them, supervising their work until they grew frayed with his hectoring and wandered off or were called away by concerned parents. When the tide encroached, Clyde flew into frenzied action, marshalling fellow sunbathers and beachcombing strangers to join the fight. He was thrilled by the waves' relentless power, urging higher walls and deeper trenches.

When the tide finally erased Clyde's castles, the tension drained from him as if a plug had been pulled. He lay back and watched the rows of curling white waves until their pattern grew familiar, then he walked into them and felt their breaking power against his chest. He waded farther, until he could no longer touch bottom and the gray peaks blotted everything but the sky. While the others beckoned from the beach, he trod water and floated beyond the surf, a blip rising and falling with the swells.

Bonnie and Blanche purchased wool bathing suits with sleeveless tunic tops, Bonnie's of red wool sporting a center front slash and tassel tie, and Blanche's, kelly green with a scoop neck and a button on the left shoulder for opening. Over these they wore linen longsleeve coverups that rimmed their knees and lifted cheekishly with the slightest gust. Blanche vamped for Buck as he snapped photos of her holding her coverup open and lying on her stomach on a towel like a pinup girl, chin on palm, cheekbones glowing, seagulls wheeling overhead. That's how it was that, in the third month of FDR's presidency, as the world's most powerful banker, J. P. Morgan, testified before a Senate subcommittee that he hadn't paid taxes for the last two years since the law allowed him to deduct capital losses; as the public wailed about economic injustice; and as more farms and businesses collapsed, the Barrow gang rubbed coconut oil on each other's arms and legs, Bonnie scrunched sand between her toes, and Clyde and Buck snoozed on towels, hands knitted behind their heads and hats over their faces.

They spent one evening drinking down two buckets of bottled beer plus all the whiskey they could find, laughing and carousing until darkness curtained a dozy stillness. In the morning, Bonnie woke to a dog lapping her foot. She kept her eyes closed, relaxing into the tongue's rhythmic slide, its slow, certain path up her sole and along her ankle, tasting each inch of skin, but when she sat up, there wasn't a dog in sight. Only the spilling surf of the melted yellow Atlantic.

Bonnie : Wellington, Texas, June 10th, 1933

When Clyde said, "Hold on to your hats, it might not have a bottom," and flattened that wooden sign at speed, I felt the wheels leave the pavement. Time did a strange thing then, it nearly stopped. I had ages to turn and look at him and say goodbye or crack a joke about him being a lousy pilot or take his hand and kiss the palm for our good luck.

The creek bank over which our spinning tires flew, though dark with night, loomed up. My cigaret lifted off the dash and hovered there, rotating one, two, three times, and I thought to reach up and pinch it between my thumb and forefinger as I began to wonder where I would first feel the pain.

My body became precious, light and whole, and I longed to keep it. I wondered whether this might be the end to everything.

I swallowed the hardness that bobbed up in my throat and bit down.

these are signs : when

a bird flies inside the house
a sash falls
a pillow keeps the head's impression
a leaf rasps with no wind
a dog howls with no moon
a buzzard shadow passes
a river glows copper
a light flickers
a dust pillar hangs in the air
a crow caws in the far away
a horse is cut by wire
a child's ears ring

many ways to know when death is coming
even more ways to die

—came to pinned under the dash smelling scorched flesh. Mine. Some later said battery acid, but I ask you this: were you there, Charlie, as the flames licked the flesh from your very leg?

The car ended up on its nose, and Clyde was outside, him and W. D. having crawled up and out the back window. He was yelling for me, and I answered.

Jesus and Mary, I'm burning alive, I'm burning to death in here.

I could hear the strain in Clyde's voice and feel his fingertips like little snails on the back of my neck as he reached through the broken window.

Shoot me, I begged. Please, just shoot me. If you love me, you'll shoot me.

His reply cut through all that heat like a piece of ice. It plunged into my ear and down my throat and erased my spine.

Baby, I aint got my gun.

W. D. Jones : Second of Six Fragments

A lawman shot off two of my fingers in Arkansas after me and Buck made a job there. There was two officers, and they run onto us accidentally as we was getting away. We had hit another car and they stopped to see about that. Buck killed one. The other run off and hid up the road on a farmhouse porch. Our car was wrecked, so we got in the police car and was about to take off when that law started firing. That man could shoot. All he had was a pistol and he was about two hundred yards away from us, but he knocked the horn button off the steering wheel with me trying to get the car turned around. That's how he got my fingertips.

Clyde and Bonnie wasn't along that time. He was taking care of her back at the tourist court. She'd been burned so bad none of us thought she was gonna live. The hide on her right leg was gone, from her hip down to her ankle. She had got hurt when we run off into a river bed where the bridge was out near Wellington, Texas. The car caught fire while Bonnie was still hung inside. It was nighttime, but some farm folks sitting on their front steps had seen us go off the road. They helped get Bonnie out, but when they seen all them guns in the car, they called the law. Clyde drew on the two officers when they rolled up, and we took their car. He set them in the backseat with Bonnie across their laps, and we drove on to meet Buck and Blanche.

Buck was all for killing the two lawmen, but Clyde, thinking how gentle they had been with Bonnie, said no. He told Buck to tie them up in the woods and we'd be on our way. When Buck come back and laughed about how he'd tied them to a tree with barbed wire, Clyde got mad. "You didn't have to do that," he said.

What lay on a pile of blankets in the backseat was a leg without skin. As the car drifted back and forth across the Texas panhandle, the skinned leg scowled and cursed and sent out dark waves of spite. The windows had to be left down for the stench it gave off, and when they stopped, blowflies formed a flag over it.

The jouncing backseat kept the leg in constant misery, so Clyde aimed north for smoother roads. On the outskirts of Fort Smith, Arkansas, he risked stopping at a tourist camp, where a dollar a day rented a cabin with indoor plumbing, a new mattress, and a pair of hot plates. W. D. was still along. Buck and Blanche took the adjacent cabin. At dusk that first night, Clyde sat peering out the window, following the cars moving past on the highway.

The leg was lying on the bed with foul armpits and unwashed hair, its dress rucked to the side. Its voice cut the air with all the smoothness of a rusty saw. "Why don't you just leave me behind? It'd be a hell of a lot easier on everyone. They'll come collect me, yall just drive on."

Clyde massaged his brow and peered into the room. "I wouldn't leave you for my life, you ort to know that by now."

Even in the relative comfort of the cabin, the leg was the worst of patients, agitated, morose, ungrateful. When Clyde ordered W. D. to carry it to the toilet, the boy hummed a radio tune or told a senseless story out of awkwardness while it cussed away; and as Blanche peeled off its soiled sleeves, the leg berated her for being too rough.

The leg saw only that its good looks were destroyed. It refused fresh bandages to stare for long hours at its craggy purple face and ugly stumps. With its skin stripped away, all that remained was raw muscle and bone spangled with nerves that flopped around and jangled against each other. It tried to recall what it felt like to be whole, but all its thoughts ended inside that tin can at the bottom of that ravine with the smell of its own pyrolyzed flesh floating up its nostrils.

It kept at hand a mirror with a smoky glass. In it, the leg watched in stages, one shifting into the next as in a moving picture of its life: the soft downy skin it sported as a youth, the shaved smoothness it knew as a waitress and newlywed, the unstroked nylon stocking it wore as a young spinster, the bare stubbled features of outlawry, the fissured skin of the crone. Curses—for those around it, for lost dreams, for Clyde's driving, for fate!—passed across its lips.

"He was her man but he done her wrong," it whispered in the quiet.

The leg's hair became an oily tangled mess. Pain creased its cheeks and collapsed its mouth. The flesh around its raccooned eyes grew withered and raw, and the irises themselves looked as cold as dead cinders. It tried to smile into the looking glass, but the result was artificial and malicious. It saw for the first time in the mirror its mother.

Once, when everyone was asleep, the leg gazed at itself and said, as if trying to convince the stranger there, "I'm Bonnie Parker. Bonnie. Elizabeth. Parker." It'd always imagined that name on a marquee, but now all that it saw were sharp edged letters cut into a stone.

Then fever set in.

June 18th, 1933

Clyde left at noon with his heart riding high and seized in his chest. Bonnie was dying. There was nothing left but to go for her sister Billie. He flew at whiplash speeds down through the Ouachitas. Hadn't eaten or slept in days. He tried to picture what life would now be like without her, and when the guilt from that effort made him feel strange, he pushed it from his mind and tried, instead, to conjure Bonnie's face, but could only make out her separate parts, an eye, a lock of hair, the curve of a breast, her nubbin toes. Where he held the steering wheel, he could feel the ghost grip of her fingers, the last part of her he'd touched.

At Jackfork Creek he veered west. Down through the Clear Boggy, his mind slipped between daydream and prayer. The tires ticked when he ran over a snake. He slapped himself hard enough to turn his head from the blow. Held his gritted eyelids open and let the brown hills crawl across the globes of his eyeballs. When his hands fell and the lids drooped, a dusky figure rose in his vision.

There, out of the forest top, appeared a shadow that darkened the sun. At Eastham there'd been a man whose bulk blotted light like that, a man who wore a toddler's dumb face and had bearlike arms garroted at the biceps by short sleeve cuffs. Hair blacked with shoe polish and center parted. Leather boots soled with three inches of rubber. Ed Crowder. One time, they were digging a ditch together, and Big Ed pointed to a mosquito biting his arm. "Look here," he said. When he flexed the muscle and held it, the insect trembled and fattened to the size of a grape, then exploded. Big Ed looked up with flecks of blood on his smile. In that voice as thin and high as a girl's, he said, "I just hate these fucking skeeters, don't you?"

The tires droned on. At some point, gibberish filled the car space. Clyde listened, trying to decipher its message. *They that wait upon the Lord shall renew their strength. They shall mount up on the wings of eagles.* Not gibberish: scripture, in his own voice. He rolled down the window and let the air blast away. Out there was nothing but dust and more dust, the covering that cloaked the defiled world in brown nothingness. He was a loser, had always been, but he would keep going if only for Bonnie. *They shall run and not grow weary,* he cried and two fisted the wheel and bore down on the horizon like a torpedo fired from a battleship.

An hour later, he was passing through the Muddy Boggy. He'd driven these drainages regular in his days before prison when he fenced autos out of Dallas. Where the land had been a green carpet, now the fields lay barren. In the mirror a cape of dust billowed and spread. A prayer occurred and he prayed it—for the prairie between the Shawnee and Chisholm cattle trails to grow dark with tombstone shadows. *Let the pestilence being drug pour into the people's mouths,* he said to the air, *and let the people be buried in great heaps in giant holes, then let the gravediggers lay sprawled over their work, dead.* The windshield glowed with the day's last light. He felt only momentary relief. He closed his eyes against the bright and saw, between the triangle of a man's legs, a river's slow glass. He felt fists plying dirt, the soil soil he'd turned over in a different life. A boot was yanking on the manacles binding his wrists. Someone was manhandling his pants. Then he was being slapped on the face, not viciously, only hard enough to bring him to.

Big Ed was starting in on him from behind, that child's voice lilting the air. "You like getting pegged, boy?"

His forearms exploded in pain as a pair of knees fell on them. A guard's face appeared, clean shaven and slick with tears, and Clyde felt a whisper on his ear. "This your first time, aint it?"

Something shattered against the car. Clyde's eyes snapped open. Outside, brimstone pits swallowed brush weed. Black trails climbed skyward. Little red birds swooped into his path and died in shrieks against the window.

His brain felt soggy, his face throbbed. Shadows grabbed at his passage. The road slipped out from under him. He watched it slide off then jump back into place then slide calmly off again before it jolted back under him. He hit himself as hard as he could, a full swing, and saw a brilliant white flash and heard sirens. His heart wobbled like a bruised fist. Flames licked the tires. Smoke filled his lungs. He calculated there were seven gallons of gasoline sloshing in the tank. Then some barrier gave way and he broke into open space. Clear sky. The horizon a jagged purple line in the distance. His lungs clutched fresh air again and again. His head cleared. In the rearvision, red barbs jumped and glowed. A wall of black smoke rose—brushfire, by God. Half asleep, he'd driven right through it. He held the wheel with his elbows and rubbed his eyes.

He made Dallas just past nightfall.

It's a story every American knows, if not in fact, then in the visible truth of its literature and in the land itself, and if in neither of those, then in the gummed eyes worn by their not so ancient countrymen. Since white settlement of the plains, plows and rustic tractors had been destroying the prairie grass, but on August 10, 1917, Congress passed the Food and Fuel Control Act and began a propaganda program aimed at getting farmers to grow wheat. The country was at war, and Herbert Hoover, the multimillionaire food administrator ("If a man has not made a million dollars by the time he is forty, he is not worth much"), guaranteed, for the first time, a price for a crop: the government would pay two dollars per bushel for wheat.

And in the decade after the Great War, the technology developed for armored tanks was adapted to the gas powered tractor, and good steel plows broke the buffalo sods in a relentless campaign to subdue the land for king agriculture. Farmers tilled all day long, then, fervent with progress, would snap on the lights they'd mounted to their tractor grills and continue tearing the earth with paired ghost eyes after nightfall. The Great Plow Up, it was called, and it annihilated in agonizing and beautiful efficiency the native web of plant roots that held everything in place in the guts of the country. The plains were remade from grasslands into a breadbasket of wheat for the entire world.

Soon enough the bill for this reckless experiment came due, as a few soil conservationists, such as Hugh Bennett, warned it would—but who had time, in the grasping for the dangled dollar, to listen to cranks and crackpots? It took the land itself to respond, and when the Amarillo black duster galloped through, it was the first of many. Over the next few years, the southern plains blew into the air, and the country passed under its black ticker tape in some dark celebration of its own destruction.

White shirt, white britches. One pair hitop brogans, nailed together. Fifty cents for a hat, a dollar for socks. Yur choice, sunstroke or rot.

Knew a guard once who hung a raccoon dick off his watch chain for a toothpick.

Ever night lying in my bunk I see a hog twisting on a spit over me. Soft plugs of meat come off in my fingers. Whole mouthfuls at a time.

Not me. Cool rivers, big mountains. I'm out night hunting pecans.

That galboy's not to trifle with. Big Ed sees you looking, he'll put you in a world of hurt.

I hear the bulls are dying for another chase team. Shit eaters'll catch you no matter how fast you run. Punch out again, yull take a walk into them woods over thar.

Come Sat'day night, ever bunk got a woman. Just listen to them springs squeak.

Them rolled britches thar, red kerchief dangling, that's Barrow, Big Ed's gunsel. Bought him for three packs of cigs. Puny little thing, aint he. Hear he's got a big pecker though. Cleans Ed's bunk so he can sleep safe. And on jack night he does what he's told behind the blanket.

Breakfast aint why they call it the Bloody Ham. Here yur alive one minute, dead the next.

Tell me. How's that so different from the rest of Texas.

4

THE RED CROWN

May 23rd

They were parked in a clearing off a wagon trace outside of Mangham, a camp they'd set up a few weeks ago when Clyde hacked away some brush with a butcher knife they'd bought off a farm wife for a dollar. They'd started the night atop a spread blanket, a tiny fire glinting off the Ford's skin and the gun Clyde was oiling and the coins Bonnie was separating into piles.

When the fire died, they lay with the earth at their backs. The trees created dark walls that made a cutaway map of the constellations, but when Bonnie thought she heard a snake in the leaf litter, she made Clyde carry her to the car, where they bedded down on an old robe in the backseat. Clyde fell asleep under a newspaper lid, and Bonnie lay staring at the dark. When the moon rose, it looked like a skull that'd been polished and oiled and set on a shelf in a dark room. Its glow fell on a headline from the *Shreveport Times* that Clyde had over his face: *Priest Urges Guillotine After Two Men Almost Decapitated at Hanging in New Orleans.*

Now, for once, he was the sluggish one in the morning. He was in an undershirt. A white silk shirt was draped over the seatback and a necktie hung from the rearvision mirror. She opened the door. "Don't mind me," she said, "just taking a little off the top."

"I think what the problem is is that I done got *too* much sleep for once," he said.

She lowered herself, one arm on the running board, one on the door, until she was squatting on her good leg. She bunched up the skirt of her dress and jimmied down her underwear and let go a hot stream onto the clover.

"The fishes thank you," Clyde said from under the newspaper.

"Oh hush. At least I'm not roaring in the rumble seat left and right like you."

Clyde sat up groggily. He moved the 45 from the back floorboard to the front seat and checked that the browning and the sawed off were still loaded. Rubbed his eyes and scrubbed his hair and ran his hands down his face.

The ground was cool with night, but the air was warm. Bonnie hopped over and lowered herself to a stump and took off her top. "Say, can you fetch my red dress from the trunk?"

"You'll want the matching shoes and hat, I reckon."

"That's how they came when they were purchased. Bring me my brush, too."

He crushed the newspaper and threw it out the window, then leaned over and waved the bees off the sandwiches in the front seat before tossing them out, also. He cursed. "What's the point of even buying something you aint going to eat?"

They dressed and freshened themselves at leisure. He brushed out her hair, and she repinned it under her hat. Then he shrugged into his shirt and fastened the buttons. Looking into window glass, he said, "I guess I don't feel like putting on my tie today."

Back in the car she looked longingly at the sandwich scatterings on the ground.

"Let me guess," he said. "You're starving."

W. D. Jones : Third of Six Fragments

I first saw Clyde Barrow under the Oak Cliff viaduct in Dallas when I was five years old. His family and my family was camped out there because we had nowhere else. Daddy had brought Mama, a daughter, and five sons to Dallas from Henderson County, Texas, where he was a sharecropper. Times was hard and lots of folks was moving off farms in them days. We finally got a house in West Dallas and Daddy went to work at an iron plant. The Barrows moved into a house down the street. About a year later, Daddy, my sister, and my oldest brother took sick and died of the flu. Mama, when she got herself out of the hospital and was well, supported us four boys as best she could. She done washing and took in boarders, and us kids did what we could to make a buck.

Clyde run with my older brother and he used to come calling on a girl who boarded at my house. He went with her before Bonnie. I was just a kid, but Clyde always treated me nice and I liked him. Then one day, his girl moved off to where her folks was in Oklahoma, and I heard he'd got her in a family way. Clyde took up with Bonnie after that.

I've heard stories that Clyde was homosexual, or, as they say in the pen, a "punk," but they ain't true. Maybe it was Clyde's quiet, polite manner and his slight build that fooled folks. Another way that story might have got started was his wearing a wig sometimes when him and Bonnie had to drive through a town where they might be recognized. He wore the wig for disguise and for no other reason.

Or the story could have come from sensation writers who believed anything dropped on them and who blew it to proportions that suited their imagination.

Some of the tales about us robbing banks all the time ain't true, either. The papers would write we was heisting a bank in Texas when we was actually off in Tennessee or somewhere else. I always figured some of those reporters was holed up somewhere with some booze during the time they claimed they'd been off with the law in hot pursuit of the outrageous Barrow gang. I

couldn't read what they was saying in the papers then, but we'd pick up the newspaper in whatever little town we was traveling through, and Bonnie would read it aloud. That way, we kept up with where the law thought we was and we'd head in the opposite direction.
Clyde always believed in being prepared. He was the quickest man I ever seen. He never wanted to kill. He'd kidnap the police instead of killing them if he could. But he killed without hesitation when he had to, because he wanted to stay free.
He was the complete boss, not Bonnie, like some have said. Clyde dominated all them around him, even his older brother, Buck. Clyde planned and made all the decisions about what to heist and when to pull out and leave a job alone.
Clyde just wanted to stay alive and free, and Bonnie just wanted to be with Clyde. He'd made the first wrong turn and couldn't go back.
He had that sawed-off 16-gauge automatic shotgun along with him all the time. It had a one-inch rubber band he'd cut out of a car-tire inner tube attached to the cutoff stock. He'd slip his arm through the band and when he had his coat on, you'd never know the gun was there. The rubber band would give when he snatched it up to fire. He kept his coat pocket cut out so he could hold the gun barrel next to his hip. It looked like he just had his hand in his pocket.
The meanest weapon in our arsenal was Clyde's automatic rifle we'd stolen from a National Guard armory. He had cut off part of the barrel and had got three ammo clips welded together so it would shoot fifty-six times without reloading. Clyde called it his scattergun. We had a couple of regular automatic rifles and some pistols. There was so many guns in the car it was hard to find a place to put your feet.
Clyde was never more than an arm's reach from a gun, even in bed, or out of bed on the floor in the night, when he thought we was all asleep and couldn't see him kneeling there. I seen it more than once. He prayed. I reckon he was praying for his soul. Maybe it was for more life. He knowed it would end soon, but he didn't intend for it to be back in prison.

Clyde :

Watched Daddy lean over Buck one time with a pair of pliers.

Holt still boy jes holt still.

Buck were on a pallet with his ankles crossed and his face in a puddle of sun.

Daddy were on a stool working over him with them knobby hands.

Buck had a nose hair was festering, and Daddy were plucking them out one at a time and taking a devilish pleasure.

Yahhow cried Buckster as true tears sprang from his eyes and he flopped around and laughed at how bad it hurt. Buck a grown man and I never seen him in such pain.

Not even that night in Denton lying on the sidewalk shot through both knees. Face bloodied from having put it through the windshield. A pair of cops coming on with guns blazing.

He yelled Go on *git*.

So I did.

July 19th, 1933

Late that night inside a tourist cabin in Platte City, Missouri, Buck was sitting on the edge of the bed, his fist inside one of Blanche's boots. In the other he held a dauber with which he was cobbing away. Blanche washed Buck's undershirt and vee line shorts in the sink and wrung them and snapped them in the air, then draped them over a chair. Her dark hair swirled about as she worked.

What she would recall speaking of in these last peaceful moments with Buck was getting away from the outlaw life and starting anew. Buck mentioned a cabin in the woods somewhere in Canada, a trade trapping animals in the winter. That life sounded so far away, she said, then asked what he'd do if she were killed in the coming days.

"What a terrible thing to ponder, doll."

"All the same, say."

"If you must know, what I would do is go on and carry your body home to its final resting place."

She gasped. "You mustn't. That's just what they'll expect. Don't ever take that chance. Leave my body someplace where they'll find it after you've gone on. Let the authorities see it back to my family."

"Now let's turn the tables," Buck said.

Blanche had her answer ready. "Why, I'd do myself in."

The dauber hung limp from Buck's wrist. "Listen," he whispered, "you've got to swear here and now you'll never do such a fool thing."

"But Bonnie has vowed no such thing to Clyde. In fact, I'm certain they swan to die together."

"That's them. Why should you be tied to my sins?"

"I couldn't go on without you."

"All the same, you have to." He paired her boots on the floor, crossed to her, and touched her cheek. "Let's not talk on it no more."

They kissed, then he undressed and slid under the covers. Blanche crawled across the bed and kissed him again. She turned out all the lights but for a small floor lamp by which she took off her shirtwaist and washed it at the sink and hung it over a closet door. She went to the window and parted the blinds.

Outside, a haze of dust hung in the air. A pair of men milled in front of the tavern across the way. One of them seemed to point right at her. Buck called her to bed. She turned off the lamp, and though she knew she wouldn't sleep, she got undressed and climbed in next to her husband. She wrapped an arm across his chest and cupped the capsule of his shoulder with her palm and lay there listening to him breathe.

In the other cabin, two untouched sandwiches wafting scents of toasted bread and soggy lettuce sat on wax paper triangles atop nightstands. W. D. lounged on the floor with his back against the wall, savoring sandwich bites between sips from a Coke he'd upended into a jelly glass. Clyde, in stocking feet and with one leg draped off the bed's edge, pored over a newspaper. Bonnie sat propped against pillows, dozing, her skin yellow and sickly, her eyelids mapped with tiny green veins. A browning automatic rifle stood in the corner, and the stock of Clyde's scattergun peeked out from under the bed.

W. D. fetched up chunks of tomato and bacon as they fell onto his shirt and popped them into his mouth while Clyde read aloud about the waitress in Tyler, Texas, who could carry twenty five cups of hot coffee at one time. Then a voice, shrill enough to pierce the walls, came from the other cabin:

"Just a minute! I'm getting dressed."

W. D.'s eyes popped. The voice was Blanche's. Clyde jammed his feet into his shoes and pressed his ear to the door.

Outside, a man in the driveway hollered, "Send out your menfolk. We want to speak with them."

The cabin had a door that opened into the garage, though Buck and Blanche's cabin had no such feature. Clyde said to W. D., "Go get the car started."

Then the voice came again from the driveway, pitched higher this time.

"You have one more minute before we start bombarding."

From Bonnie's Journal :

The camera shows the front of the cabins. This is Platte City, Missouri, at the Red Crown Cabin Camp (change the name if the owner offers trouble). An armored car rolls up the driveway, and about twenty laws creep up behind it. They're in mortal fear because they've heard who's in the cabins. Some of them carry metal shields. They all have guns. The gang is inside, sleeping.

But one of them is not sleeping. Jack Bailey is looking out through a crack in the blinds. In his arms he holds a subgun.

Next, the front of the cabins again. Suddenly the *rat-tat-tat* of a subgun explodes from a window. The gunshots pour out. Now they come from the front door. Next, the garage. It's all Jack, but the laws think they're facing an army. They run for cover behind the armored car.

The laws' voices
> By God!
> Fall back!
> They're killing us!
> It's a deathtrap!

A tear gas bomb sails from out of the dark and hits the roof. Jack opens the cabin door, raises the subgun to his shoulder, then blasts the armored car.

The laws run for their lives. They cower behind the corner of the tavern.

Jack turns to the gang and says
> Get in the car!

The gang piles into the Ford. As Verlin and Ida run across the driveway, the laws finally get off some shots. Bullets cut the air. Verlin shouts and falls.

Ida screams

Help me. They've shot my Verlin. Please help me!
Jack lets go a withering stream of gunfire. He storms
out to his brother and drags him to the car. The gang
pulls him inside. Jack jumps in.

The laws reload and aim their guns at the idling car.
After a moment, it roars out of the garage. The laws
unleash one last barrage of bullets. Glass shatters.

Ida screams in pain. She says over and over

My eyes, they got my eyes.

The car roars off down the highway. The gunfire stops.

> *. . . aw, hell's bells, it's too much even*
> *for Hollywood! They'd never buy it!*

It was the back roads by which they vanished after Platte City. When the skies opened, they drove on into the rain. Blood and upchuck pooled in the floorboard. Blanche held Buck's head on wadded newspaper in her lap. Window glass in the final fusillade had shattered in her face, and she felt as if she had frayed wires in her eyes. Clyde went all out until he was certain they'd crossed the county line, then he stopped along a country road. They had passed out of the rain onto dry ground. He took Buck by the armpits while W. D. grabbed his legs. Blanche kept her hand pressed to Buck's head as they carried him to the front of the car and propped him against the fender in headlamp glare. When Clyde lifted away Blanche's hand, he groaned.

"Jesus," W. D. said.

Unable to see, Blanche felt for Buck's hands and, taking them in hers, clenched them to her chest. "How bad is it?" she said.

Bonnie wrangled her way out of the car and hobbled up. She looked on in grim horror. A thick red stripe marked Buck's scalp line above which, dangling from loose cords of hair, were gems of tissue and dried blood. Inside a rictus of gore on his forehead, a button of brain fixed them with a gray eye.

Clyde said only that they had to tend to one thing at a time. He gently took Blanche's face in his hands and leaned it back into the light, then pried open her eyelids. He pinched the largest shards from the humors and flicked them into the dark.

Blanche remained stoic throughout, not even a whimper, and afterward she knelt there in the road, her dress heavy with her husband's blood and his head like a stone on her thighs. She pictured her weak hearted father reading in the papers about her part in a gun battle. Years later, in her memoirs, she would confess that this was the darkest moment of her life, that she wanted to press her head against Clyde's pistol and ask for a final mercy.

But Buck's chest was still rising with breath.

"We've got to get him to a doctor," she said.

Clyde said that turning him over to the authorities meant a death worse than one on the road. If the state did heal him, he explained, it would only do so in order to run electric current through his veins. This was a certainty, given their crimes. "You'll suffer a million times more if you let them destroy him that way." He studied the ground and gazed up at gray clouds blimping past the moon. He was twenty three years old.

"I'd rather we both die in prison than end like this," Blanche said. "I don't care what happens to me, but don't let him die like this."

Then Buck moaned and asked for water, but there was none to give. He was surrounded by the four of them, Bonnie against the fender, Clyde and W. D. bent over, hands on knees, and Blanche on the ground, holding him. In that small stain of light pushing back the raven dark, with a bullet having drilled through his brain, from within the surety of death, Buck said, "We won't give up. We keep on driving."

Platte City, Mo., July 20—A Texas paper has commented in an uncomplimentary manner upon the Platte County officers allowing the bandits to escape. We must all confess it looks strange that four people surrounded in small cabins by thirteen officers could get away, but the breaks came in favor of the bandits just at the right time and it seems to us no one is to blame for the escape, unless it be the Kansas City officers who bungled things with jamming guns and an armored car without much bullet resisting armor.

The bandit battle was a great celebration for the Red Crown and came upon its second anniversary, being just two years to the day the tavern opened for business. The cabins, with their bullet marks and shot-up interiors have been visited by thousands.

Clyde : Dexfield Park

when that Ford we had since before Platte City hung
up on that goddamn stump we all piled out and I felt
one on my cheek like a switch another in my arm like
a wasp in muscle meat then pellets going up my back
and when I saw a mans head turkey up out of the grass
I lifted the pistol with my unkilled arm and emptied it
while the others made for higher ground

my cheek fell open and I thought I might leave half my
face in Iowa but it only hung there wet and stinging
and I kept going and when I got to Bonnie theyd shot
her twice across the stomach and she were bleeding
something awful then a bullet knocked the boy down
then Buck fell again but we kept finding our feet and
crutching on rifles into deeper brush while bullets
slapped trees and chunked dirt

we made it over a rise and through some bracken and
there we were a ragtag party stumbling along and it
were something that morning with the dew rising off
the hillside and the sun pouring down and the river
below glowing copper and us running through the
woods bleeding like stuck pigs

Buck said yall go on I cant do it no more and we couldnt
carry em both and I knew theyd be hunting us and we
had to cross that river somehow and somewhere find
wheels

Buck had a few shots left and I had the boy reload my
45 with the seven shells from my pocket and I looked
up and the leaves on this tree were glowing like the
first color of green and I started praying Lord mine
enemies pursueth but you goeth before them will you
help us get out of this one and take from me this yoke
of choosing from between Bonnie and Buck

but that were the Lord speaking to me in my own words
you have to choose Clyde Barrow you have to choose
its gone be either lover or brother you cant keep both

so what do you think I done?

the current pulled the blood coming off us downriver
and the kid toted Bonnie with her dark patch showing
on that wet nightgown and I later looked it up on a map
and found that this were the raccoon river and when
we got up that bank and come up on a farm I told the
boy walking there that I didnt want to kill his dog but
I would if he didnt call him off and told him the law
had done shot the hell out of us up in the park and we
needed a car and that was just one of the many times
the Lord ushered me from a fix

but he were true to that first choice because Buck and
Blanche done got cornered and them laws peppered
Buck to hell even with his head bandaged from the
bullet he took at Platte City and then they put him
in that hospital where Mama came and held his hand
and watched the spit stretch between his lips and the
law asked him all sorts of questions while his brain
sat there leaking and bloody rheum on his face but he
didnt tell em nothing they didnt already know and then
he slipped into a coma and then he died

In Des Moines Blanche was fingerprinted, booked, and stood atop a scale on which she registered eighty pounds. Her eyes were cleaned of most of the glass and the more damaged left one wrapped with a makeshift cotton and tape patch. Then she was led to a dimly lit room with two chairs and a table, where she waited in the stifling heat for several hours, fighting the urge to tear off the eye bandage. At one point, a portly man in a dark blue suit with matching Eleanor blue tie and pocket kerchief entered and introduced himself with a long title. He had a round face and tiny white hands.

It was late afternoon. The room was so hot that his face grew a garden of sweat, but he kept at the interview for two hours straight without removing his jacket. He would pause in the questions only long enough to sop his face and neck with a white handkerchief that he pulled from a black leather case he kept inside his suit.

All the while, with her eye throbbing and itching, Blanche bandied between claiming ignorance and giving false names that the man scribbled into a notebook with a pencil. Finally, she gave the real name of a smalltime crook whose path the gang had crossed months earlier, Hubert Bleigh, and though poor Hubert would be arrested in Oklahoma within days, it was a false lead.

The interrogator sensed as much.

He took out a sharpener and spun the pencil inside. The shavings purled up and fell from its razor edge to the floor. He brushed himself off. Said he wanted Clyde Barrow, his habits, his likely location, his main contacts. Said this was her last chance to come clean.

He stood up and walked behind her. When he tucked a loose strand of hair behind her ear, she flinched. "I never did ask," he said. "How's that eye?"

"How do you think? It still has glass in it."

He curled his fingers around the pencil, then cupped his other hand around the back of her head. "I meant your other eye."

For a long time, she sat there staring at that pencil point. Finally, her interrogator shrugged. Disappeared the pencil into a pocket. Gathered and slid his notes into a folder, and, without looking at her, left the room.

Blanche was transferred to Platte City, where she pled guilty in Circuit Court to the charge of assault in the Red Crown gun battle. On September 4, 1933, Sheriff Holt Coffey, wearing fresh scars from Clyde's browning automatic in that battle, escorted her to the Missouri State Penitentiary for Women in Jefferson City, where she was received as prisoner number 43454. Early in her decade long sentence, she had a series of surgeries on her injured eye, but eventually its sight was lost.

The Wall Street bandits
In their lust
Have trampled the people
Into the dust.

They have robbed millions
Of all their feed
In order to gorge
Their sordid greed.

They have robbed the populace
Of their home
And put them out
On the earth to roam.

They have gathered wealth
In great big stacks
And piled up debts
On the peoples backs.

In this grand style
They live at ease
They fear no law
And do as they please.

And the man who robs a country bank
He only robs by retail
These bandits who in millions rank
Rob by slaughter wholesale.

If hailed into court
By the powers that be
Most of our courts
Just set them free.

—Texas poet Cyclone Davis

"About three o'clock on a long summer day, de sun forgets to move and stops. Den de mens sings dis song."

Bullies, if you work, I'm goin' trust you well.
An' if you don't, I'm goin' give you hell.
Oh, Hannah, go down!

You orta come on dis river in Nineteen-fo',
You'd find a dead nigger on ev'ry turnrow.
Oh, Hannah, go down!

You orta come on dis river in Nineteen-ten,
Dey was workin' de wommens like dey was workin'
de men.
Oh, Hannah, go down!

Go down, old Hannah, don't you rise no mo',
Oh, Hannah, go down;
If you rise any mo', bring Jedgement Day,
Oh, Hannah, go down!

—Iron Head, convict number 3610

5

GRIT

May 23rd : Bonnie

Off the back bumper a gloved cross floats, a black four fingered hand that grows in the mirror each time Clyde taps the brakes.

I close my eyes, then, when I open them, there's a truck with a wheel off.

The cross comes tapping at the windows. I rub my eyes to see past all the flying glass.

The cross touches Clyde in the temple. I reach out to hold him, but one of its other arms has me pinned against the seat.

The cross makes a crowd of the place. I sigh each time it pushes in.

It counts coup on me again and again.

No number can contain it.

Nothing is worth this.

Then outside Amarillo one night the pair pulled over to witness sudden white wires walking under the belly of a black thunderhead—

—the weeks since Dexfield had been spent recuperating as they crisscrossed the back roads of the nearby patchwork land. It was a dry and monotonous country seamed with sandy waterways. At sunset one day, an enormous flock of black birds scared up from the roadside and schooled overhead, and where the sun caught them, their bodies flashed silver. The sight was so extraordinary that Clyde pulled over, and they watched the birds become a roving waterlike shadow in the sky that rose and swooped and fanned and shrank as a single fluid unit. Bonnie pointed and described the shapes the flock made, ocean wave, box, bottle, lilac bloom, and her mood was such a change from most twilights that they sat parked until it became too dark to see.

After Wellington, riding in the car meant misery for her. Both feet swelled, and the only help was hooking them on the dash and making a waterfall of her dress, but that soon rendered them numb. Sundown was the worst time of day. With a crime magazine she'd read umpteen times ramped on her knees and her cheek mashed against the seat back, she would stare out at the ruined fields from which every stitch of life had been scraped and find there a well of emptiness that matched her own. It was as if two mirrors with nothing between them but their own empty frames had been set face to face, and what resulted was a pair of endless regressions of emptiness. On the day after the flock of birds, as she sat thus at twilight, the sensation grew so frightening and it so paralyzed her being that her mind, in a pulse of self protection, sent her out from herself. She looked down on top of the Ford, its windows burnished by the setting sun, and on winged thoughts flew to where a low cloud might pass were the sky not an endless brown swirl, and only once did she feel a stab of panic recalling Enoch's translation, but assured, an instant later, that she of all women had failed to obtain a testimony that would invalidate her appointment with death, her flight continued, pleasure rising with height, until the Ford grew so motelike that it no longer showed any forward motion but merely twinkled there, distant and small, the way a tiny ring of gold, dropped into a pond, would, through dark layers and surface ripples, catch the light and signal its presence.

They kept driving, up through buttes and tilted highland valleys scorched with the sun's heat. The car, like all their cars, wore a skin of dust. They entered one of those towns where buffalo hides had lain in stacks as big as railroad cars, one after another, not two generations back. They passed farms reclaimed by dust dunes, the crooked and collapsed pickets of fence lines rising from golden grama their only guides. At twilight, they parked in flats beside scrub oak, where dust blasted the car and they could see nothing save the tablets of brown the windows became. They would wipe their faces and feet with wet rags made from flannel shirts, then lie beside each other in the backseat. Bonnie held a pencil above a notebook, and she couldn't have seen what she wrote had she tried, but she wrote nothing. Instead, she listened to the wind and sensed in its movements the way the car shaped itself around her. She could feel its tires rooted to the ground, its parts rising from the axletrees. She thought of herself as a doll inside a shell, the air inside the doll gone stale, and the doll's nostrils hardened with dust.

She woke to a figure standing over her, but it was only Clyde's suit coat draped from the window crack. The sky's dark cast and the window edges worked on her mind. She could close her eyes and still see the colorless screen hemmed behind them. West of Lampasas scrolled black dwarf mesquite and, in the bottomlands, green sutures of timber into which they drove, and there, having stopped, they moved finally from the car and made beds of gathered grass and slick pine needles, Clyde's arm enwrapping her and a too thin blanket failing to hold their heat.

They spent August wandering, too, recovered enough to begin robbing again, a filling station or shop every other day or so according to need. The boy performed the gun work while Clyde monitored from outside and Bonnie lay in the backseat, ready with preloaded hardware. Outside of town, Clyde would send W. D. shinnying up a telegraph pole with a pair of wire cutters. He'd come down with his hands and thighs porcupined with splinters and a grin made wicked from fear.

They would ride for eighteen hours straight, baking under the sun's lens during the day and freezing through night's endless chill. Their backs kinked, their bird dogs ached, splitting pains erupted behind their eyes. Dallas began to feel distant and unreal, and they stopped speaking of their families.

Days, Clyde would gaze across a featureless plain wobbly with heat waves and nod off and forget that he was supposed to be keeping them balanced on the strip of blacktop until the tires bumped off the road edge, hurling dust into a sudden canopy, the springs banging and squealing and he'd think, *I almost just killed us*, and an instant later, *What would it matter if I had*, and he felt so small and insignificant under that sealike boundless sky that it didn't seem possible he'd killed half a dozen men or was feared by a single soul anywhere.

They traveled country where stones knuckled from the ground, where, in place of cattle, swollen stomachs teetered atop stick legs. Strange visions appeared: Carthaginian pillars rising off windblasted fields; black rags swirling atop an oak tree; a ring of kneehigh demons tugging golden gobs from a carcass; an eagle madly flapping its wings, struggling to lift off with a human leg locked in its talons. A narrow back road drew them through an empty town, where roof shingles curled like dry leaves and the buildings were pocked and peeling as if from a great heat: a drugstore, a cafe, a teacherage, a Masonic hall; and on the outskirts, just off the road, a hand cranked cotton gin dissolving into simpler elements.

In a German dairy town, they risked stopping at a Catholic church, and Clyde carried Bonnie to see the egg blue interior and soaring arches and idolatrous figures. While W. D. kept watch outside, the lovers found a stone bench inside a grotto and there gazed like schoolkids at the virgin's blank eyes until they were overtaken by a sacred feeling. By then, Bonnie was more skeleton than flesh. She sat with her mortified leg across Clyde's knees, and it felt like anything could be said in the cool damp quiet of that place, as if they'd stepped into the caveworld of the dead.

"It seems like so long ago," Bonnie said. "I used to sit at home wondering if I'd ever see you again. I used to worry it wasn't me you wanted, that you'd left for good, then I'd fight that feeling by playing sieve and shears and featuring you strolling in the front door and smiling at me in that easy way you have. I'd go back and forth like that all day long, and it was like the sun passing in and out of shadow. You've been my world for as long as matters. I wasn't anything before I met you."

Clyde moved his hat from the bench to the ground. His face was a doughy mask with an ell shaped stitchery of dark thread under the left eye where he'd sewn himself up after Iowa looking in the mirror. He pistoned his knuckles along her arm. "Some things don't do to say in the open air, honey."

Her words sounded like fervent prayer, they came out so rushed. "I don't care, I don't ever want to stop feeling this way. It's the truest thing I've ever known. I've been a ruined woman since I was sixteen." She glanced at the holy figure and her cheeks flushed. "I'm flighty and emotional and scared to pieces half the time. And look at me"—she held up a wrist—"nothing but skin and bones. If we couldn't be together, well, I'd no longer want to live."

"I hate to bring you down, too," Clyde said, "but it fairly inverts me to think of you with someone else."

She laced her hand inside his, said, "You're the only thing I ever want anymore. The best way is for us to stay close until the end."

The light was blue, the color of sunrays passed through ice, and where it touched his swollen cheeks and nose, it gave his face the quality of having been carved from some stone locked away inside a glacier. "That's how I see it," he said. It was a vow they'd made before, but saying it in this place felt like consecration.

From then on, he kept driving them toward whatever the horizon held, the notched peaks of distant mountains, a lone butte, or nothing at all but an indistinct blue line. Bonnie resettled into the road life. In early morning coolness, with the windows up, she'd sit near him, stretching her neck so that her eyes shone back at her in the rearvision and brushing her hair until it flowed around the tines like taffy. Hills slid past, brownocean swells that lifted and lowered them.

Blistering along a deserted caliche road one afternoon, with Bonnie dozing in the passenger seat and the boy doing the same in back, Clyde selected an approaching road sign. As he neared it, he stood on the brake and cut the wheel left. Then he released the brake at the same time he pulled on the hand brake and swung open the door. The result was that the Ford pirouetted under a mushroom plume of dust, and as it came to a stop and his passengers jolted awake in flailing, stupored awareness, he slid from the car like oil being poured, one bent knee coming to rest on the road's crown, as the browning in his arms winked open and aerated the sign's face with fat lipped holes. As Bonnie swore at him from the window, Clyde had the boy make a picture of him standing beside the sign with his fist shoved through the largest of the holes.

Bonnie's wrath didn't cool until that evening, when they came to the enormous escarpment known as Caprock, the eastern edge of which they traced past motts of black limb trees. As night fell, Bonnie held Clyde and W. D. spellbound with one of her grandfather's stories—of Indian mustangs herded up the nearby cliffs and slaughtered during the Comanche War, and of sightings in the century since of ghost herds galloping the rimrock on moonlit nights. Her listeners pressed their faces against the windows and gazed up at the black ridgeline.

The next morning, they sidewindered up the stair step, and the visible world flattened into a panlike monotony that opened without end and was broken only by far between canyons and shallow valleys. The land was peopleless except for a single farmer sitting a tractor, a momentary insect crawling between eroded gullies.

Here they found a deserted farmhouse, one claptrap among many, and they nailed sackcloth over the windows and made themselves at home. Gray wood peeked through rippage in the newspaper glued to the walls, and while Clyde massaged his stocking feet and W. D. lay on his back gazing at the ceiling, Bonnie read from a section on the wall that dealt with the reinterment of Thomas Edward Ketchum in Clayton, New Mexico:

> *"Black Jack Ketchum will be remembered by longtime readers as the train robber who, on the morning of his execution, dashed up the gallows steps and called, 'I'll be in hell before you start breakfast, boys.' These readers will further recall Ketchum's capture in the year 1899 after a failed robbery and his attainment of true fame when he was mistakenly decapitated at his public hanging.*
>
> *"Breathing life back into Black Jack's story was the New Mexico Supreme Court's decision earlier this year to strike down the law of 'felonious assault upon a railway train' as unconstitutional, leaving Mr. Ketchum's relatives free to petition to have his remains transferred to the Clayton Cemetery.*
>
> *"Time and limestone have been good to Black Jack. His suit was in prime condition and his black mustache was as bushy and full as ever in life. Before his initial burial on Boot Hill, his head had been sewn back onto his body, and the parts seem to have agreed these three decades, since the stitching has held."*

Clyde's laughter started slow and grew into a gutlurching honk that incited Bonnie, too, so that she had to struggle to finish the piece between bouts. Then they were laughing at each other's laughter, Black Jack's tale forgotten.

W. D. was propped on an elbow outside the lamplight circle, his gaze pinging between them. "That's plain gruesome." When tears began running down their faces, he sat up with real concern, beholding them as if they were the writhing victims of a nerve gas attack. "I don't hardly see the humor."

This only made it funnier. When he could, Clyde said, "No, you wouldn't," which brought a new upswelling from them both.

W. D. stood, embarrassed for the pair, and headed for the ramshackle kitchen. "Yall need something to eat, I reckon. The road's done made you antick"—

—and as they watched the storm from Amarillo's purlieus, they sipped whiskey, some of the finest they'd ever tasted, purchased from a good contact on town's edge. This was in the late summer of 1933, when they had less than nine months to live. W. D. had dropped out, so it was just the two of them. Bonnie had hunted the car over and found only a battered tin cup to pour it into, saying, as she did, "This'll have to do."

Clyde took his first sip, closed his eyes, and managed only, "Wooeee."

Bonnie's sip caused a low hum to stir in her throat that purred and fizzled into a slow sigh. "Not exactly ditchwater, is it?"

The whiskey was sweet and smoky and smooth, and for as long as it sat in the mouth and on the tongue, it brought pleasure. They'd come upon something pure—and though it had no greater meaning beyond the hereandnow, that was enough. Its lack of meaning was, fact of business, what gave it such worth.

Bonnie exhaled through her nose. "You know what some people might say? That this would taste even better out of a fancy glass." She smacked her lips. "Shit, I'd drink this stuff out of my shoe."

Clyde didn't need to respond. They sat sipping slowly for a long time in the silent dark, watching the laddery white strikes—

W. D. Jones : Fourth of Six Fragments

Bonnie was always neat, even on the road. She kept on make-up and had her hair combed all the time. She wore long dresses and high heels. She was a tiny little thing. I reckon she never weighed more than one hundred pounds, even after a big meal. But them big meals was usually bologna-and-cheese sandwiches and buttermilk on the side of the road. Run, run, run. At times, that seemed all we did.

Bonnie was like Clyde. They had grit. They meant to stay free or go down together. She was always agreeable with him, but they did have some fallings out. I've seen them fall out over a can of sardines. He jerked it out of her hands and opened it with his pocketknife, and her trying to tell him it had an opener.

Sometimes when she got puffed up about something, Clyde would kid her and say, "Why don't you go on home to Mama, baby? You probably wouldn't get more than ninety-nine years. Texas hasn't sent a woman to the chair yet, and I'd send in my recommendation for leniency." She'd laugh then and everything would be smooth again.

Bonnie smoked cigarets, but that cigar bit folks like to tell about is phony. I guess I got that started when I gave her my cigar to hold when I was making her picture.

Them little poems Bonnie made up made the papers, too. She would think up rhymes in her head and put them down on paper when we stopped. Some of them she kept, but she threw a lot of them away.

Bonnie :

There's lots of untruths to these write-ups,
they're not as ruthless as that.
Their nature is raw,
they hate all the law,
the stool pigeons, spotters and rats.

They call them cold-blooded killers,
they say they are heartless and mean.
But I say this with pride
that I once knew Clyde,
when he was honest and upright and clean.

But the law fooled around;
kept taking him down, and locking him up in a cell.
Till he said to me,
"I'll never be free,
so I'll meet a few of them in hell."

W. D. Jones : Fifth of Six Fragments

We never wanted to kill nobody. But during the time I was with them, five men got it. Four of them was lawmen shot in gun battles.

We was hit, too. Sometimes we was hurt so bad it seemed like the end. I got shot in the side at Joplin and my belly ached so bad I thought the bullet had stopped there. Clyde wrapped a slippery elm branch with gauze and pushed it through the hole in my side and out my back. The bullet had gone clean through, so we knew it would heal.

I reckon most folks find it hard to believe we never went to no doctor, but that's a fact. We stole a few doctors' bags out of cars and used the medicine. And we bought alcohol and salves at drugstores. But we couldn't risk going to no doctor.

I left Clyde and Bonnie after they was healed up enough to get by without me. Clyde put me out to steal a car up in Mississippi and I hooked 'em back to Texas.

I'd had enough blood and hell.

She moved the air
with a handheld fan
fluffy white clouds
across ricepaper folds

At sunset they sat
atop the prairie
and suppered on fatback
white bread and beans

In the long blue evening
they didn't speak
then night drew slowly
down its salted walls

    How long to go on this way?
    Hard to say
    I sure miss my mama
    Well who don't

She lit a cigaret
and blued the air
and snapped ash the way
a bird dips its beak

    Always dreamed
    of seeing New York City
    You're in luck
    it's just around the corner

He unbreeched the shotgun
and checked the load
    We'll cruise Broadway
    and look at all the lights

The next day they nooned
along a dusty creek bed
having bought canned
peaches off a farm wife

To his mouth she fed
syrupy a slice
catching in the cup
of her palm the drips

Healed, they made the trip home, where they kept close to their families, spoking outward in daylong jaunts. Bonnie put on some weight. Clyde's did, too, but he also became quieter, jested less, lost track of conversations. Memories of Eastham still cindered him, and he couldn't go a week without waking at least once with his fists clenched so tight his fingernails left bloody smiles on his palms. A trip through the Ozarks had put him in mind of joining forces with someone buried in a place so deep in the hills they'd never be found. With the right partner, they could hit the prison, then retreat into green oblivion. He began leaving Bonnie with different family members and at Dallas hideouts while he made the underworld rounds, using his outlaw fame to reconstitute a gang.

The Joplin police had found a roll of undeveloped film in the gang's effects left behind at the garage apartment, and it was these photos, especially the one of Bonnie smoking W. D.'s cigar with a 45 held brazenly against her hip, that, when broadcast across the nation's newfangled wire service, propelled them to outlaw celebrity. Bonnie, the married woman who ran off with a fugitive, and Clyde, the Texas Rattlesnake, became common fodder around the supper table, when families bartered story for story, and conversation paused only long enough for the essential truth of each tale to take hold before someone else shook her head in wonderment and recalled something she'd read or heard and contributed another tidbit. It was a story yet without ending, so tellers naturally focused on its beginning: Henry and Cumie, it was generally agreed, were goodhearted folks who'd done no more than try to provide for their own. What led their sons to turn outlaw was a system corrupt from root to stem—*venality sown, vengeance grown*, as the preacher's saying went.

A historian would write, "Virtually every bank that was robbed in Depression-era North Texas testified that Bonnie and Clyde were the culprits as if this was a badge of honor." Yet, in another way, their notoriety was a boon. Hatred of banks, businessmen, the government—and, by extension, its officers of the law—the very forces, it was perceived, that had stripped the people from the land and the land of its wealth, shielded Bonnie and Clyde. Restaurant owners who'd given food and dishware to a young welldressed couple refused to talk with officers; farmers who'd chatted with a group camped on their fields failed to call the authorities when they heard about a nearby robbery; witnesses to the robberies themselves clammed up. In northeastern Oklahoma, Clyde robbed a filling station attendant of eight dollars and asked him kindly not to report the crime; returning several days later, having scanned the papers and found no mention of the deed, Clyde handed the man a hundred dollars. Earned or not, what stretched over Bonnie and Clyde was a Robin Hood cloak pleated with class fealty.

Reinforcing this silence, of course, was a fear of retaliation. Bonnie and Clyde drove faster cars than the law and carried bigger guns. They were known to have cruel natures and to be endowed with supernatural powers of detection and reach. It was commonly assumed that they would hunt down stooges without mercy, that every other person on the street might have some secret connection to the pair. Within their home territory, it would take someone with diminished loyalty and a reckless hubris to put them in real jeopardy.

Joe Bill Francis was a West Dallas delinquent and friend of Clyde's younger brother L. C. The young lurdan was roughly built, with edges to his muscles and a high horseshoe forehead. Pus filled bumps speckled his face, and a "bile," as he called it, swelled on the back of his neck to the size of a prize marble. He wore his wavy dark hair thick with brilliantine, had familiar ways, and jested coarsely in front of girls his age. He liked to idle around the Barrow station, where much of the days were spent in speculation about the health and whereabouts of the Thomas Howards, the name by which the family referred to their outlaw relatives—that being one of Jesse James's aliases. To others outside the family circle, Joe Bill bragged of his close connections to the Barrow gang.

When L. C. acquired a motorcycle, he and Joe Bill took turns riding it at evergreater speeds along the deserted roads west of town. One day, the two of them rode it out to a family meeting next to an open field. There, in the cool fall air, Clyde decided to test the contraption. The boys were filled with helpful tips.

"It don't steer like a car, more like a bicycle."

"Pull the choke if you feel her chugging."

"But keep your speed in turns so's you don't stall."

"And don't snag your trousers on the magneto bolt."

The boys ran in escort with Clyde as the motorbike teetered and accelerated. Once it straightened, he opened the throttle and roared off. Joe Bill whooped from within a cloud of brown exhaust.

"I bet he masters it his first ride," L. C. said.

The rider grew pinlike, and after he passed the vanishing point, the boys stood there, suddenly stripped of purpose as the engine's hum diminished. They shook their heads and traded grins and kicked the dirt.

A few minutes later came a gunshot pop. L. C. and Joe Bill jumped into the family sedan and tore off. As they crested a hill, they saw the motorcycle on its side in the ditch, Clyde pinned underneath. L. C. skidded to a halt.

Clyde's face was tomato red by the time they got to him. He was waving a pistol, shouting, "Get this goddamn thing off me."

The boys grunted the motorbike upright. Joe Bill was too stunned even to help Clyde dust himself off. "I can't figure it," he said. "Nobody can match your driving."

"That may be," Clyde said, stumping around on his sore leg, "but after this, the only thing I'm driving on two wheels is a car."

By then, Billie Jean's children, Buddy and Jackie, were four and two years old. Jackie was too young to have memories of her aunt, but Buddy recalled Bonnie fondly and would pat his younger sister's head when she was snubbing and say, "Don't cry, Jackie. Never mind. Aunt Bonnie's coming after a while and sing the crawdad song."

Bonnie saw her nephew and niece during the

roadside visits. She would mug Buddy and clasp him to her and bounce him on her good knee and lose some years singing and clapping with him. On the drive home after one such outing, Buddy turned to Emma and said, "I shall tell my mother I have been with Aunt Bonnie but nobody else." Emma patted her grandson's head and told him what a good boy he was.

On October 11, Jackie took suddenly sick with a stomach disorder and died two days later. Bonnie collapsed when she heard the news. That weekend, the same ailment struck Buddy, and he was taken to Bradford Memorial. When Clyde and Bonnie pulled up to Emma's house on Wednesday morning, she was sitting on the front porch steps. A wail broke from Bonnie at the first glimpse of her mother.

"Don't say anything," Bonnie cried. "Buddy's dead, I know it. I dreamed it last night."

"I started to buy toys to send him," Clyde told Emma, "but she wouldn't let me. Said she knew he wasn't alive no more, but I didn't believe her."

Emma's mouth cemented into a frown. "The babies are both gone now," she said, then reported on Billie Jean. "All she'll say is, 'It's hard to tell if life's even worth living anymore.'"

In the weeks that followed, Bonnie wore only long dresses cut from dark cloth, and she stopped using makeup except for eyeliner. Her hands flitted as if under a nervous spirit's control. Her eyes grew red spider webs. She became helpless, despondent, pathetic. If she at times found a cheerful mood and returned to being the dramatist, adopting the cornpone grin of the filling station attendant or the woozled speech of the cafe waitress who kept forgetting their order, these episodes relied on a strained jollity and merely set in relief her overall state of deterioration. She spent as much time drunk as possible, had to be carried from the car over any significant distance, seemed unable at times to distinguish between dreams and reality. She constantly held her face in her hands. She complained of portents and bad dreams. Strange pains dogged her. On some days, she seemed unable to hear people when they spoke, as if she were in a well and their voices shouted down. At the sight of a child, she'd weep without comment, though if the reports of her pregnancy are to be believed, it was during this time that she conceived a child with Clyde.

When they were parked and Clyde sleeping, she'd write a pages long letter to her mother, her sister, a cousin she hadn't seen in ages, lighting one cigaret off another, monologues about her life recorded in beautiful penmanship. She imagined herself as the unappreciated artist, the vilified cynic. Once, when Clyde woke and asked what she was writing, she lit the pages on fire and held them out the window. They transformed into a glowing swarm that rose to the treetops, and she said, "The dregs."

On another afternoon, as they drove a treeless stretch between west Texas towns, where the horizon was disturbed only by knobs of barren sandhills, she looked up from a newspaper article about the government's plan to squash the Middle West's crime wave and said, as if suddenly cheered by good news, "Think of it, honey. They're going to machine gun us, those officers. 'Stoo bad, aint it?"

Her eyes retreated inside their darkening frames. She slept fitfully as Clyde drove, and when they stopped moving, her mind snapped awake. She kept her group of gangster poems she'd begun in the Kaufman jail as close as Clyde kept his guns, and she constantly escaped into them. She liked to start a poem violent and quick, then progress it into something slow and filled with sorrow. When she spoke, it was to recall with sentimentalized nostalgia her girlhood spent with Billie Jean and cousin Bess. She considered her mother sacred, a greater and greater symbol of lost purity. If Clyde looked over and saw the inky sheen of mascara on her cheeks and asked what was wrong, she might say, "How do you think those people keep from rolling out of them slanting houses?"—and even in these altered moments, she'd look at him with such trust in her eyes that the laugh rising in his throat would fizzle before it could escape.

In early November, they drove east from Dallas across the treeless black prairie with its scatterings of limestone rubble, and Bonnie summoned the schoolbook creatures she said inhabited the ancient sea of that place, finned dinosaurs, clams as big as dinner plates, sea turtles the size of houses. There was a shark so big, she said, its eyes were wider than tractor tires, each of its teeth taller than a lamppost.

Across the Sabine, they entered that part of Texas wild with speculative oil frenzy, where sharecroppers who'd been leading quiet farming lives found their towns overrun with wildcatters and roustabouts, conmen and prostitutes. Where the red dirt hills had once been blanketed with towering oaks and sweet gums and the pecan trees strung with grapevines, now the woods were crisscrossed with muddy roads. It was a country where federal inspectors were routinely run off with shotguns and sometimes killed. They passed pools of gray mud used for drilling and they skirted trenches of black mud angling from hot oil operations directly into streams. Shacks ran more parallelogram than rectangle and housed families who'd taken in roughnecks and roustabouts, letting them sleep in back rooms and storage spaces, hallways and barns. Fields that had grown corn and wheat three years ago lay fallow. Peach orchards were rutted from heavy equipment. Trees had been cleared—and the wood used to build the derricks that infested the hills and were attended by trucks and antlike workers. The boomtown of Kilgore bristled with so many derricks that a person could walk from one edge of town to the other by stepping across drilling platforms and never have to touch a sidewalk. Clouds settled low over the place. The bustle of men and machines filled the air.

The Jim McMurrey Refinery was a small operation in the heart of this country. On November 8, none of the truck drivers or workers at the refinery paid much attention to the woman who pulled into the yard, looked around, then drove off. She returned a few minutes later, this time with a man who stepped out and approached the group of big bellied men standing outside the office. The size of a junior high kid, he wore dark glasses and brandished a pistol. "Get your hands up," he said and nodded them inside. Jim McMurrey, plant manager Ray Hall, and the truck drivers did as they were told, then made themselves into curtains against the office window.

The gunman motioned toward an eight inch pipe sticking up from the concrete floor that had a hinged lid secured with a padlock. He said cordially, "Open it up or give me the key."

McMurrey said he didn't have the key, though it was on the ring at his hip. The gunman showed no sign of belief or disbelief, merely held the pistol to the padlock and fired two shots that roared pain into the men's ears. The bullets whanged around the office, and the big men ducked and threw their elbows up around their ears. The gunman opened the lid and pulled a wad of bills from the pipe. He said, "Thank you, gentlemen," and made his exit.

From the window they watched him jump into the passenger seat and roar off with three thousand of the company's dollars.

Dungaree America :

Stripped bare meadows no longer feel the plow
but push crops of cocklebur and catchfly
while the river flows in a trickle line
and turkey buzzards lord from their towers.

The mossbacks in this country make nothing.
Lawyers, politicians, carpetbaggers,
and public servints nick ever comfort
while it's him with the shovel makes something.

Two things catch ever one, gray hair and death,
yet while we live a family must eat.
The devils in Washington call us hayseeds
as starvation pay sinks us into debt.

Each week we punch a new hole in our belts.
What we want is life, Mrs. Roosevelt.

The first time an Eastham inmate tried to escape, he would receive a beat down with pistol handles and be dressed in stripes; the second time, after recapture, he would simply be led into the woods by a pair of guards and shot, a practice called spot killing. The guards would agree that the prisoner had attempted to run, then they would claim the twenty five dollar reward for having prevented an escape.

6

SOWERS

May 23rd

Q. Now then what did Barrow and Parker do after you left them in Shreveport?

A. They went back down looking—

MR. MASON. Objected to unless he knows of his own personal knowledge.

Q. Now where did you go after you left?

A. To my brother's at Castor.

Q. Where did you go from there?

A. I stayed there.

Q. Did you in the meantime contact your parents?

A. I had already fixed it with them the night before.

Q. When was Barrow and Parker killed with reference to that day, the day you left them?

MR. MASON. Objected to: Incompetent, irrelevant and immaterial, unless he knows of his own personal knowledge.

Q. Do you know of your own personal knowledge when they were killed with reference to the day you left them in Shreveport?

A. The next morning.

The longer Clyde Barrow and his cigar smoking gun moll, as the newspapers called Bonnie Parker, stayed free, the more those same papers painted Dallas County Sheriff Smoot Schmid as inept. Schmid found himself tied to Clyde Barrow from the very start. Five days after taking office, on January 6, 1933, Schmid authorized two Dallas County officials to assist in a midnight operation designed to catch an unsophisticated bank robber named Odell Chambless, who reportedly had plans that night to visit a safe house in West Dallas operated by Lillian McBride, one of Ray Hamilton's sisters. Five officers hid in the dark, awaiting Chambless at Lillian's house, when Clyde Barrow happened by instead.

It was dark when Clyde approached Lillian's porch. Ray Hamilton had been arrested again, and Clyde had stopped by to verify that Lillian had smuggled hacksaw blades to her brother in the Hillsboro jail. As Clyde neared the porch steps, a curtain hem moved in the front window and he opened fire. The officers shot back. Two rushed up from the side of the house. Clyde leveled his shotgun and killed Tarrant County Deputy Malcolm Davis, a veteran officer, with a blast to the chest. Then Clyde vanished like smoke into the night.

Schmid at first thought Chambless was the killer and made the mistake of saying so to the press, but when it came out that Chambless had been in a Los Angeles jail the night of January 6, the newspapers turned on Schmid. He next claimed that Clyde Barrow was the likely culprit, while another deputy mentioned the killer might've been Pretty Boy Floyd, said to be operating in the area. At a press conference, a reporter asked Sheriff Schmid whether Jesse James oughtn't also to be scrutinized, his having been dead half a century only partially disqualifying him as a suspect. Schmid raised a white flag hand and walked stiffly out of the room.

After that, the first duty in the sheriff's office for Ann Turner, the secretary, and Ruth Cox, the chief administrative deputy, was to compile any new information on the Barrow gang. Ruth would gather the overnight dispatches while Ann walked down the hall to the holding cells. There, from a wire tray on the night guard's desk, she would retrieve the stack of clippings from the day before. Schmid had ordered the county jail inmates to scour the region's newspapers for possible references to the Barrow gang and to clip these. Ann glued the stories into a black scrapbook so large that, when open, it covered half of her desk. Then the dispatches and scrapbook were handed to Bill Decker, the unassuming chief deputy who quietly ran the office's operations and whose recommendations Schmid inevitably took. Decker would study the latest material, cull the pertinent items, and at nine a.m., report to Schmid on any new leads.

On the morning of November 14, 1933, Sheriff Schmid fumed in his office. He drummed the closed scrapbook with the fingernails of one hand, while holding, in the other, a typed warrant. Across from him sat Ted Hinton and Bob Alcorn. Schmid's face, with its haggard resolve, still wore the moony openness that, along with his unoriginal campaign promises—cut budgets, get tough on crime—had won enough voter trust to give him a tight election. The state had axed $15 million from its budget, and Schmid's first decree as sheriff was to reduce the total county payroll for deputies from $90,000 to $80,000 while hiring five new officers. Alcorn and Hinton, two deputies suffering under the belt tightening, sat with their hats propped on their knees. In the last meeting like this, Schmid had swelled and hinted at a run for governor if they could stop Barrow, but all morning he'd been stewing over Decker's latest batch of reports.

"Let me be frank, men," Schmid said. "It is my intention to capture Barrow and his moll. Do you understand?"

Alcorn shifted in his chair. "With all due respect, sheriff, that boy is not ever going to give himself up. Ted and I have seen what he's capable of in Joplin and in Iowa. It will not matter how many officers surround him or how many guns are pointed at him. He will turn tail every time."

Schmid pulsed his jaw and looked at Hinton. "Ted, do you share that opinion?"

Hinton nodded. He had a wizened, Italianate face that was handsome despite its excessive length. A lean nose and offset eyebrows. Folds creased the skin of his cheeks, and purple half rings lurked under his eyes. He drove the Dallas streets nearly every night, keeping lookout for the outlaws while his wife, pregnant with their first child, sat at home. People thought every Ford V8 with a young couple in it was Bonnie and Clyde, and he and Alcorn had chased down dozens of tips. Like the pair they hunted, the officers slept in the car or sometimes didn't sleep at all. Hinton spoke in his slow manner. "Yes, I believe that boy would fight a buzz saw."

Schmid fanned through the scrapbook and chewed his lip. He held up the warrant. "William Daniel Jones is in Houston. Five nineteen Franklin Street. Now I want the two of you to go down there and pick him up. Put the screws to him if you have to, but find what is needed to get Barrow dead to rights. Then we will corner him and he will have no choice but to surrender."

Alcorn said, "I will arrest the Jones boy, Sheriff, but getting the drop on Barrow won't be as easy as it sounds."

Hinton pinched his hat by the taper and placed it on his head. "He just isn't someone you come up to and say, 'Stop, in the name of the law,' and slip handcuffs on. Clyde Barrow has already killed enough people. There's no reason to give him a chance to get the drop on us."

Schmid leaned back, palms braced against the desk edge. "Listen here, I want this criminal brought to justice, not killed outright. I intend to march him and that wayward woman down Main Street. I want to show the world what I have done."

Schmid stood.

He was a head taller than most men and had earned the nickname "Bigfoot" for his size fifteens. He handed the warrant for W. D. Jones's arrest to Alcorn, then shot his cuffs and neatly sat back down, though his chair gave an indecent squawk. "I appreciate your thoughts, gentlemen, I truly do, but we'll do this my way."

On November 16, Ted Hinton and Bob Alcorn arrested W. D. Jones at his mother's house in Houston. Under interrogation, W. D. said, "It's hell out there, just hell. Never sleep in a bed, never eat a good meal, always running scared, never knowing when a bullet is going to catch you. God, I'm glad to be in this jail. Don't ever make me leave it while Clyde's alive."

He narrated his months riding with the Barrow gang and, every so often, pulled back a shirt hem or rolled up a pants leg, showing them by the end seven bullet scars. Jones gave a signed confession of three typed pages in which he claimed not only to have been the gang's hostage, tied to trees at night, but to have been incapacitated—asleep or unconscious—during all the gun battles and kidnappings. In each killing he fingered Clyde as the gunman.

Just as Clyde had coached him to.

November 21st, 1933

The mothers prepared a meal to celebrate Cumie's birthday. Mrs. Barrow killed and fried the bird she'd been saving and baked a tin of sweet cornbread. Mrs. Parker made stewed pokeweed, red beans, mashed potatoes, and a pecan pie. The families squeezed into Joe Bill Francis's sedan, where they spread a blanket over their laps on which they held a peach crate packed with the food and a gallon jug of sweet tea.

On the drive, Emma was quiet. She gazed out the window, looking on the sights Buddy had called out when he made this same drive with them not two months ago. Two dead grandchildren. And now her own troubled child falling away, the child for whom she felt the most tenderness and into whom she'd poured her greatest hopes. She touched the ragged edges of her hair in back. There was no time to sit in a beauty parlor. That morning, with her sewing scissors, she'd lopped off a finger width of hair all around, including her bangs, chopping them into an awning that said grief, grief, grief. When would God show some mercy?

Her mind still failed to accept what the papers

told her weekly, that her daughter was the outlaw companion of the Southwest's most notorious gangster, someone she couldn't help but think of as a skinny boy with elephant ears whose face dimpled when he smiled. She knew that her daughter felt insanely toward Clyde. It was that feeling, call it love or what you will, that drove Bonnie to fashion herself into a criminal: it was the only way she could be close to her man.

The money Bonnie pressed into her palm from time to time brought little relief, though Emma had used a portion of the most recent handoff to buy the girl a red silk dress with a spilling vee neck and raised velvet shoulders at Titche Goettinger's. She carried it now, wrapped in brown paper and tied with twine.

Along deserted Highway 15, in what was then the open country west of Dallas, the families parked the cars nose to nose. Bonnie held her mother and sobbed. The two of them were in the sedan's backseat. Emma helped Bonnie out of her old cotton dress and camisole until all the girl had on were what she childishly still called her underscanties. The girl's face and hands were sun darkened, the rest of her skin translucent and pale. The purple corkscrew of Bonnie's left leg was familiar to Emma, but she hadn't before seen the pair of pink okra pods that looked like they'd been embroidered with an unwieldy needle below the girl's sternum. Emma touched them lightly then stepped her fingertips up the scale of finer scars lining her piano key ribs. "Creation, Bon."

"You should've seen the blood, Mama. It was pure gruesome."

Emma's voice strained. "You've done given this boy your body entire. I can't see why you go on like this. I wish you two had never met."

"It's no use second guessing fate. We'll just be together until the end finds us."

"But what can death mean to people as young as you two?"

Bonnie pushed her head through the scrunched up portal of the silk dress. Emma helped her wriggle it on and straighten it, then took from her purse a box, which Bonnie opened. Inside, she found a necklace with three silver teardrop pendants.

The girl flushed. "Oh, it's beautiful, Mama! You oughtn't to have bought me anything, but I'm glad it was this."

"I just wish you would come home."

Outside, Clyde's youngest sister Marie had spread an oilcloth over a flat patch of ground and was unpacking the food. Billie sat with her knees together on a corner of the cloth and stared off, watching the sky change colors. L. C., whom the family called Flop for his ears, which stood out even more than Clyde's, upended the peach crate for a rickety stool. Joe Bill squatted on the bare earth and watched Marie pour the tea into canning jars. Cumie rested her feet on the other sedan's running board, settling in sideways on its backseat and surveying the gathering with palsied nods.

When Bonnie emerged, she showed off her new necklace. The group fell silent as Cumie said grace, then Emma guessed portions and filled plates while Marie waitressed. When Bonnie took a bite of red beans, she sighed. Her eyes grew wistful.

"Now don't be dauncy," Emma said. "I cooked those special for you."

"Truth is, I could eat a nation of them, but they make me so sad now. These were Buddy's favorite."

Everyone looked to see if Billie would flinch. But for a trembling lower lip, she was still, staring blankly at the plate atop her knees.

"Sometimes neither of us feels much like going on," Emma said. "I'm plain carved out empty."

"Thing is," Billie said in a voice that a small breeze would've erased, "I've lost my babies. I don't want to lose my sister, too."

The Barrows showed a sudden interest in their plates. The only sound was Joe Bill's cracking the tendons on a chicken thigh. Bonnie shrugged and said, "Well, why not? Why can't we parley about it? There's no use acting like we don't all know how this is going to end."

"I wish you would think of me a minute," Emma

said. "Here I am, a widow who's lost her grandbabies. When we drove up to Iowa, I spoke with those farmers who carried you across that field. I figured you were off in the woods somewhere, dying like a wounded animal. I thought I'd lost you. I'm sorry, it preys on me."

Cumie umhmm'd and added, "It preys on all of us, it do."

"That posse in Iowa shot us to pieces," Clyde said. "They filled us full of holes. But we got up and kept going. We was bleeding so bad when we swum that river, we done turned it red."

"I'm one helluva swimmer," Joe Bill said and stripped a bone clean with his front teeth. "'Scuse me, Mrs. Barrow, Mrs. Parker, but I am *something* in liquid."

Bonnie aimed her fork at Flop. "You two got some arrangement here?"

Flop shook his head, but Bonnie squinted and seethed. "You're fixing to foist another huckleberry on us, aren't you?"

Flop said, "Joe Bill's straight off the Devil's Back Porch."

Cumie spat. "I don't care for that term or for any mention of Old Scratch for that matter."

Bonnie pinned Joe Bill with a look. "Some fall a ways off the porch, I reckon," she said, and when the boy ducked and glanced away, she nodded and said, "This chump hasn't got the stuff to ride with us."

"Let him be," Clyde said. "I aint looking for another duffer just yet."

"I say and still believe the boy's afflicted," Bonnie said.

Joe Bill sleeved chicken grease from his chin, but a flicker of the hand was all Billie wasted on the sideshow. She persisted. "Mama's plain frantic for news about you, Bonnie. Aren't you afraid of what waits around the next bend, over the next hill?"

"Of course I'm scared. But none of us knows what any day holds. The only difference is, with us, the bogeyman's there day and night."

Emma held up both hands. "Why would anyone want to live like that?"

"Sounds kindly exciting," Joe Bill said.

"Oh, shut up," Billie said, "what do you know?" She plucked a handkerchief from her dress pocket and wiped her eyes and failed to register the spite on Joe Bill's face. "Do you want to know what Mama does first thing each morning? Hunts the paper front to back before she even perks her coffee, then wants me to read it through in case she missed some mention of the pair of you."

Bonnie set her plate on the ground and hugged herself from a chill. At home when she was younger, she would often make her mother breakfast, then go around the house after she'd left for work, picking up her mother's nightgown and slippers, stroking them and cooing to them as she returned them to the closet. Marie scooted over and rubbed Bonnie's shoulder. Bonnie said, "Don't mind me, I just got an eye winker is all."

"I feel like I'm being punished," Emma said. "That I don't know how long my punishment will last or even what it is I'm being punished *for*. What if you did come in, honey? Blanche only got ten years. Why would they give you more?"

"Because I've *done* more, Mama. Blanche was scared out of her wits the whole time she rode with us. Wouldn't even touch a gun. Not me. I know it pains you to hear, but I've done some very bad things."

Cumie claimed the difficult silence that followed by honking into a yellow rag. In her face's terraced hide could be read her decades as a farm wife. Her outsized eyeglasses framed raisins ("I am in good company," she'd say, "ponder your Galatians Six"), and as she spoke, her chin danced to its own rhythm. Responding to the unaired query—*What ailded you?*—she cataloged a litany: poor sleep, lethargic bowels, hip pain, gas pains, weak ankles, rheumatism in her hands and feet. Trials that she folded into the troubled lives of her children as she developed an impromptu devotional.

"Why are the poor made to suffer?" she said and peered at each of them in turn. "In your ancient scripture, you'll find that the people of Shechem desired a head man. Just where do you think they gone first? Why, they went to the olive tree. It didn't want nothing to do with them, so they went to the fig and so on. This is a parable. These trees were righteous men who knew their purpose was to produce fruit, not to king others.

"At long last, they approached the thornbush, and it were the thornbush agreed. The thornbush, you see, was Abimelech, a wicked man as ever lived. Well, what were the first thing he done? I will tell you. He lit fire to that tower with them people inside. Then he destroyed that city entire and done poured salt over its ruins."

She found application in those who hunger after power, in the voices that prop them, and in the systems created to berm their dominion: that is to say, in the officers who hounded her boys from the very start, in the newspapers who labeled them "no accounts" and "that Barrow bunch," and in the Dallas police and the upstart federal agency she'd begun to hear about. "Man is ever short of the glory of God and his will too readily warped by the lust for power."

Clyde was looking at a portion of the sky, where a set of jaws was being painted sheer red. The jaws grew out of a wispy cloud in the shape of a bird's body, its wings sprung from its sides with the effort of swallowing what looked like an enormous egg. He finished sopping his plate with a piece of cornbread, then, as if in reluctant complaint, picked up the subject of power and weighed it, asking whether each person isn't appointed some little power, even if it's only a child's mashing of an ant under a fingertip. We all face choices, he said. It seemed at first that he was speaking of the same men as his mother, but before long it became clear that the person he had in mind was himself. "I reckon it's only natural to want to test your God given powers. Buck used to say you aint broken the law until you're caught. I do know this much. When I bought my first speedster for fifty dollars and saw how fast it could go, boy howdy, I run like nobody's business. But it weren't no fun unless the big sticks had a chance, so I'd give em a glimpse. They'd take the bait and come on. I guess it's nice to think that I was forced into it, but it were just for sport."

"Once you make their short list," said Flop, who'd had his own troubles with the authorities, "they never forget your name."

"One thing do lead to the next, I reckon." Clyde began mumbling about Eastham, sinking under the weight of his words, until he emerged the way he might up out of water into bright air. He took a breath and cast his gaze around. "All that's ancient history now. We run to keep running, that's all. There just aint no other way."

"Step on the gas and kick her in the ass," Flop said. Clyde grinned at his favorite saying. "So long as there's a pedal underfoot, it don't matter so much. Say, in the Walls, there was a con who refused visitors once he got his date with the hot seat. Couldn't bring himself to see his family no more. I get skittish each time I think about never seeing yall's faces again. But when we're together like this, I feel natural, ready to take on whatever comes my way. One part of me wants to keep quiet so we can have more nights like this." He drained his tea, then looked softly at his mother, the dying light on her face, and found the force to add, "But I admit, another part of me wants to blip em back."

Flop and Joe Bill prodded Clyde for details. He joked and said, "You egg me toward ill," but by then was unable to resist giving the names—Henry Massingale, Dock Potter—of men with whom he'd been speaking about a raid on Eastham prison. He said there was another man who'd also been on his mind, that they'd just that day come from Oklahoma—and that another visit there, to the eastern parts, would soon be in store.

Billie's face took on ferocious life. "You mean to contact that Floyd character?" Her eyes jetted flames, her fury having smoldered all during Clyde's talk. Her resemblance to Bonnie magnified to startling effect, and the heat passing between the sisters disturbed the air. "Maybe you two missed what happened in Kansas City this summer." She turned on Clyde. "You'll be the death of her, goddamn you."

Clyde couldn't hold her gaze, but instead looked out over the field. "That's what I keep telling her. She ort to come on home and leave me behind. I wish you'd convince her likewise."

Bonnie scoffed. "I couldn't do it, not now. They'll keep up the chase till they put us in the ground—"

"Till a grave cools us," Clyde said. Before supper, he'd arranged with his mother to have GONE BUT NOT FORGOTTEN cut into the stone over his and Buck's grave.

Emma looked up as if she might respond, then Marie, who'd been studying her shoes, jumped up and said cheerily, "My, haven't we grown morbid."

"And this on Mrs. Barrow's birthday," Bonnie added. "We ought to at least be happy about that. Let's celebrate us being together."

As Marie bussed past, girlish and flouncing, Clyde grabbed her wrist and wound her into him. He buried his nose in her neck as if she were a decade younger, and said, "You sure stink pretty, Sis."

She squealed and nearly dropped the plates. Told him insincerely to quit it, then glanced at Joe Bill, whose gaze swirled with envy and admiration.

Clyde gave his head a wet dog shake. "Well, aint I been a big old loomp. Here I thought this kid was just hanging on Flop. You're after bigger fish, aint you, boy?" He nodded at Joe Bill, then squeezed Marie's ribs and said, "What'd you do to make him so love drunk, chew heart leaves?"

But she only said, "Hush," and swatted his shoulder.

As if Joe Bill weren't right there, Cumie said, "Yammer yammer all day long with her girlfriends about that boy. I don't know why we put that instrument in, I can't hardly keep the line clear for business—"

"Mama, please."

Cumie waxed motherly as she adjusted her hat in the back. "So long's they don't go parking in the river bottoms where them nigger brothers killed that poor white girl."

Joe Bill piped up. "Mam, you can rest easy on that point, I'll just tell them who Marie's brother is," which got some laughs.

Clyde stretched his arms overhead and permitted himself a playful feeling, easy and without the taint of recent troubles. He'd grown stronger in these months, his shoulders bigger from carrying Bonnie, his chest expansive. He said, "Outlaw fame aint what most people expect," and lightened the mood further with a story of stopping at a sandwich joint and of the car full of boys who pulled up alongside, joking about gangsters. "One of them pointed and said, 'Look, there's Bonnie and Clyde right there.'" Clyde reported calling the loudmouth over and ratcheting his hogleg in front of him and saying, "'You can close your face and keep it closed, feller. I *am* Clyde Barrow and this *is* Bonnie Parker, and if you mention our names again, we'll drill you full of holes.'"

"That poor boy's jaw fell as slack as fruit," Bonnie said. "He was so scared, he couldn't take nary a bite of his sandwich. Just sat there sucking air while his buds ate."

When it came time for goodbyes, Clyde held his people in long embraces and called himself a heel for not having brought his mother a birthday present. Nothing Cumie said could assuage his guilt until she agreed to meet the next night in the same place, this bit of information being overheard by all.

Earlier in the evening, when Charlie Stovall had noticed two cars parked on his land beside a grove of his persimmon trees, he grew suspicious because that particular location afforded expansive views of all approaches, but when he paid a visit, parking his truck and walking up on them with a hard stare, he found a family gathering, the folks friendly and carefree, and he thought no more of it.

That is, until the next day, when the Dallas County sheriff called and asked permission to carry out an arrest on his property. Sheriff Schmid explained that he had just received word that the Barrow gang would be meeting again in the same place that night. The mothers were to be driven there by an unnamed informant who'd been with the group. (This, of course, was Joe Bill Francis, whom Marie would later marry and divorce). And would Mr. Stovall mind nailing a tin can to a fencepost along Sowers Road at a point that would afford cover for a group of officers?

Bonnie :

The summer I was sixteen
Billie and I rounded up
the neighborhood babies
and carried them to Granny's.

Not many know I lost a baby
with my husband Roy
when I was seventeen.

Mothers pushing strollers
carve rivers of pain.

The pain splits in two,
branches that island my heart.

They were pretty as a picture
lined up on Granny's porch,
black and brown and pale,
eating ice cream we'd phoned in.

It was a morning in August
when I gave Roy the good news.
All he said was, I'll be a dirty name.

The mattress was floating, the pillow,
ice. Mama was there, and both of us
were saying, My baby, my poor baby.

How come Clyde aint bigged you yet,
people say. Now maybe they'll shut up.

Billie gave a penny to Sam,
the drugstore delivery boy,
for bringing the ice cream so quick,
then we fed them babies till they got sick.

Clyde :

That Sowers field was black as coal where them laws lay like matchsticks. We had a purse tied with red ribbons in the backseat for mama.

Our mothers waited in the parked car watching for our headlamps. When we pulled up the law started popping shots.

Bonnie stomped the footfeed and I leaned out the window with a 45 in each fist and fired at the muzzle flashes and swore to end each and ever sonofabitch who dared put our mothers in such peril.

On the road over I bulldogged an oncoming coupe and blasted its windows. We rode sitting on glass.

Bonnie woozed then me too and we felt our legs but found nothing.

When we stopped for gas Bonnie poked her head out. There hanging from the running boards were the red ribbons from mamas purse. But wed done left that in the other car.

It took weeks to heal up.

This is what the law did. Punched the dirt and swore at Ford steel and cursed the peashooter rifles they held and listened to the sound of our motor fade.

This is what I did. Parked outside the courthouse and watched for Bigfoot. He never left that place for lunch he werent hemmed in by three or four lackeys.

When Nellie found out what I was planning she liked to snatch me baldheaded.

It were one of them nights parked outside the sheriffs house watching his bedroom light snap off my pistol warm in my hand under a newspaper that I decided what was needed was a bigger strike. He never did come out and look at the moon.

A lizard tastes the air with its tongue, rabbits chew late season shoots, bats slurp insects from the air. The pair sit on the steps of a shanty in the woods and watch the dying red sky. Their legs are wrapped in dirty bloodstained bandages, the edges of which they worry with fingertips. In the distance a motor putters.

When it grows cool, he helps her inside to a soft chair. Scutched corn cobs and broken glass lie piled in the corners.

He batches some kindling under a piece of coal in the stove and lights it and collapses on a tick by the window.

Bonnie listens to the kindling crackle as she falls asleep. Footsteps on the steps startle her awake. The sides of the barrels between her and Clyde glow red.

The burlap curtain swishes aside, and a man appears. His lantern throws swooping shadows. He swings the light over Clyde and jabs a fingertip into his cheek, frowns when he doesn't wake.

The man opens a cupboard and produces a tinted bottle, which he uncorks and tilts into his mouth.

BONNIE. That aint jittersauce, is it?

MAN. Course it is.

She takes the proffered bottle. Her first swig returns a little, and she puts a hand to her mouth.

BONNIE. Goddamn. It's hot as Hades. What is it?

MAN. Pure corn.

She rinses her mouth with another swig, then runs her fingertips daintily over her lips and hands it back.

The man moves slow. Bullish shoulders, blue serge slacks, clean white shirt, dark tie, two tone shoes. A thick upper lip gives him a brooding look, but his strongest feature is his massive skull, square at its corners and topped with a black helmet of greased hair shaved to the skin from around the ears. His eyebrows tighten into ridges that cast precise shadows across his forehead's enormous plain.

MAN. You two can't stay.

BONNIE. Charles Floyd, I presume?

MAN. You bring too much heat. When your old man wakes up, you got to hike it on out of here.

BONNIE. Glad to know you, Mr. Floyd.

FLOYD. It's nothing personal, but I'm not one to put my family at risk for someone who operates like him.

BONNIE. And how might that be?

His eyes are sunken and dark. When he speaks, his gold capped teeth look like they're chewing a tiny fire.

FLOYD. Just bird work. Fleeting and flying all over the map, jumping states every day, doing gun work for grocery money. No mam, no thank you.

BONNIE. I didn't realize people in these parts were so hospitable.

FLOYD. Show up here again and I'll have my people call the Tahlequah sheriff who's a personal friend, that's what I'm telling you.

Bonnie hikes up her dress, exposes the white flesh of her good leg and the bandage with its dark stains.

BONNIE. They just about picked our bones clean outside Dallas last night.

FLOYD. It will happen.

BONNIE. All the jobs they think we've done have got them madder than hornets.

FLOYD. By now they've accused me of everything except taking the Lindbergh baby.

BONNIE. Funny, I'd already chalked that one up beside your name.

He looks at her blankly. She fluffs her dress hem.

BONNIE. Did you know, Mr. Floyd, that it takes more muscles to frown than it does to smile? I see you like the hard route.

He moves to the stove and takes a slow sip.

FLOYD. My partner always used to say that trouble hangs on a woman's skirt.

BONNIE. Seems to me trouble hangs on just about

anyone outside the law. Or anyone who doesn't have obscene amounts of wealth.

FLOYD. Wealth is wasted on the wealthy.

BONNIE. It's cozy and all, but this place is hell for service.

He retrieves a blueglass jar from off the shelf. Blows the dust from inside, pours two fingers, and hands it to her. She takes it with a feminine nod.

FLOYD. When I wrote to the governor, I told him that I have robbed none but the monied man and that is true. It was all bonded money and no one ever lost anything in any of my operations except the big boys.

BONNIE. Clyde's not one to chase after riches, that's for certain.

FLOYD. No, you two are hardly more than petty cutpurses, I guess. It's all them photos made you famous.

BONNIE. We were just sporting.

He moves to the window, brushes the glass with his knuckles.

FLOYD. Nah. I'd just as well get the goods as have the name. When I got out of serving time in Jeff City, I didn't figure to go on with life of that kind, but every place I went, they dogged me. I got as far away as Colorado, but they picked me up and charged me as a vagrant. And for my troubles I expect to go down before too long.

She sips the liquor with canny eyes that say she contains mystery and intelligence if he will only bother to notice.

BONNIE. If you don't mind my asking, what is it that made you start down the path to perdition in the first place?

He glances at her to see if she's baiting.

FLOYD. I'm the only one of eight kids to choose this line of work. I've refused my brothers every time one wants to join up. Someone might say it's because I was born a rebel. Maybe that's true. I do remember this. One year at revival, I pulled a boyhood prank. The babies had all been put in the carriages to escape the heat inside the tent, and I got the idea to switch them around. This one here, that one there. When the meeting was over, everyone went on home. It liked to take a week to get all them baldies back with their rightful folks.

Bonnie laughs then claps a hand over her mouth. They glance at Clyde, but he doesn't stir.

BONNIE. Why, you're a subtle genius.

FLOYD. I see something pure in my mind and then I have to create it. That was a case of once having conceived of the possibility, I couldn't *not* do the thing. I always been like that. What I call necessity, others call criminal.

Floyd takes a draw and holds her gaze. She throws back her drink's remnants.

BONNIE. I don't really see how you and Clyde are so different. He's fixing to pay some of the bastards back.

FLOYD. We *are* different, I tell you. First off, I don't carry out operations with a woman for a partner.

From her poke she takes a cigaret and a gold tipped match that pops when she lights it. She pitches her voice so low it wouldn't disturb a lace veil over her face.

BONNIE. Sometimes I can't tell the difference between being in love and being in pain. You and I will never know each other intimately, so I guess I'll speak freely.

FLOYD. Be my guest.

BONNIE. Here's my sad story, Mr. Floyd. Everything was so wonderful before the laws hauled Clyde off. Then we ran together for a time, and they started calling me a wayward woman and locked me up. After that I swore that I'd go straight. But what kind of normal life could I have had after seeing the other side? Who wants a gangster's girl? I'm speaking openly and I guess I don't care. What brings me pleasure comes with a hell of a lot of pain.

Smoke rises from her cigaret as they consider the red light on each other's face.

BONNIE. But you've got larger things on your mind. You were speaking on the outlaw nature, and here I am, giving you a schoolgirl's troubles.

FLOYD. Darling, you can unravel your troubles to me all night long. It's a rare thing in my experience to come across a female so deeply felt. I never agreed with my partner anyhow. I've always loved women myself. Can't get enough of them.

BONNIE. Can I tell you this? You'd be surprised to hear it. Sometimes I wish Clyde and I had never met. There, you got me to say it, the one thing I was most afraid to admit.

FLOYD. Hell, sometimes I wish I was more like my brothers with their farm wives and kids and plows.

BONNIE. Who can say, but if I'd never met Clyde, I'd never have taken to the road. Horrible things have happened to me because of him.

FLOYD. I enjoy women the most when it's new, when everything's off to a fresh start. Take Ruby and me. You couldn't imagine our passion in the first days. Things burned hot. But I'm not one to tarry. I quickly grow bored.

BONNIE. Maybe that's a man's way, but Clyde's never even looked at another woman so long as we've been together.

FLOYD. Shit.

They watch as Clyde rolls over.

FLOYD. If that's true, why aint he bigged you yet? Did they make a woman of him in prison? Or maybe he keeps a dwarf heart. Myself, I like every type of woman, tall, short, fat, thin. And I like to have them every which way.

His eyes move over her at last, guiding ropes binding and pulling her close.

FLOYD. Say, why don't you throw off this chaparral punk and come over to my side? You and me could have some fun.

She squints and pulls smoke into her lungs. As if on cue, Clyde stirs and sits up. Her face breaks like a mask, and she erupts with sharp cries of pleasure.

BONNIE. You *must* think I'm a schoolgirl, Mr. Floyd. Don't think I'm not flattered, but you couldn't fathom the bond we have. Did you know that we share his prison disease? The truth is, the more you suffer, the deeper you feel, and I've suffered more thinking he might die before me than I have from any bullet.

FLOYD. Aren't you something.

Floyd leans back, drains the bottle. The lines on his face distort to fiendish effect.

FLOYD. So he's your god, is he?

BONNIE. If you don't cotton to it, I don't hold that against you. You've got the set up here, Mr. Pretty Boy, tucked away like a hermit in these hills. Can't throw a stone without hitting a kin. Eyes for fifty miles. You know hours in advance when the law's coming. You're two counties away by the time they arrive.

CLYDE. What is it I've missed, a friendly feud?

FLOYD. Listen here, they want to exterminate me. They call me a mad dog. My work feeds a dozen families hereabouts. I keep the country school in fuel during winter. I tear up first mortgages when I find them in the paperwork. I've got babies named after me. What banker can make those claims? I don't know what you two birds stand for, but I stand for freedom for me and them I love.

CLYDE. I see you two have met.

FLOYD. No bank wants to be robbed by a nobody.

CLYDE. Course not. The sons of bitches need us more than they'll ever say. They got to pin it on a name they know.

FLOYD. The Hoovers of the world tout one kind of harmony, with them on top. And the Roosevelts tout another, where we're all standing in the soup line. The preacher, well, he offers a third way for storing up treasure. I'm a godly man, make no mistake, but I'm an earthly one as well. I've got to have my taste while I'm still around.

BONNIE. It's a lovely philosophy, aint it, Daddy? Spartan like.

FLOYD. People say they're on our side against the banks, but when they fill me with lead, those same folks'll turn right around and say, *See? Crime don't pay.*

BONNIE. They'll wag their fingers at our funerals.

CLYDE. Outlawry's the only thing comes close to freedom in this country anymore.

FLOYD. I bow and scrape to no one.

CLYDE. They're so afeared of people like us that they make us out to be an invading army. They've got me down for so many things, I can't keep up. So I'm thinking, why not give them something to write about after all.

FLOYD. I want no part in it, do you hear me? I want no part in your scheme.

Floyd stands and replaces the bottle in the cupboard, then picks up the lantern.

FLOYD. How long do the pair of you intend to dawdle here?

CLYDE. Say the word.

From the doorway Floyd regards them as the light gutters.

FLOYD. My pappy allus gave aid to anyone in need. I know a doctor in Muskogee who'll stitch you up. Beyond that, I'm no help.

He sweeps away the curtain and passes through. The light's edge flickers under the burlap hem.

Houston, Apr. 5—Lee Simmons, manager of Texas, prison system, today favored "more axes, if they need them," for convicts who mutilate themselves to escape work or punishment.

Simmons declared it was preferable to let "a few convicts bang themselves up" than to allow them to escape "to bang up the public."

"As long as they want to do that," he said, "I say give them more axes if they need them."

He said he regretted that such things occur, but that prison officials were determined to prevent escapes.

"Every time one chops himself in an effort to get out of work or to create sympathy for himself," the prison head asserted, "he's going to be kept right on the farm. And when he's well he's going to be put back to work on the farm. That's the way to stop that."

7

LEX TALIONIS

May 23rd

He wiped the dew fogged windows with an oil rag that trailed wet beads, then helped her out into the cool air. They were screened from the dirt road by trees and brush.

The sun was just beginning to warm things. Birds flitted from branch to branch. A bobwhite sang its name. It was a pleasant feeling, the sense of getting in on the early part of the day. Bonnie set her hands on her hips and arched her back and looked up and there would've seen a mouth carved in the sky by the trees and brush.

They drove into Gibsland from the east. At Ma's Cafe they stopped for sandwiches, then took Ringgold Road south. They passed the church; they passed the graveyard; they passed more trees and brush.

The day was cloudless. The sun had just cleared the treetops. Up ahead two swampers rode atop the logs in the back of a flatbed truck. They crested a hill. On both sides of the road were trees and brush.

I, Major J. Crowson, being of sound mind and memory do hereby make this my dying declaration, to Gordon M. Burns, notary public, and at the time of making this dying declaration I am conscious of approaching death and I believe there is no hope of me recovering and I am making this statement voluntarily and not through the persuasion of any person and this declaration is not made in answer to interrogatories to lead me and I am telling the truth, the whole truth, and nothing but the truth, so HELP ME GOD:

I am called at the Eastham state prison farm "Long Arm Man" or "Backfield Man," and on the morning of January 16, 1934, Olin Bozeman was carrying No. 1 squad. I was riding a horse and I was in front of Bozeman's squad. It was about 7:15 a.m. when Bozeman called me and said, "Raymond Hamilton has jumped in my squad," and I said, "Boy, that is for something," and Bozeman said, "Yes it is." Joe Palmer was in Boss Bozeman's squad and he pulled an automatic pistol. It was a .44 or .45, and Joe Palmer shot me in the stomach. After Joe Palmer shot me in the stomach he shot at me once while I was riding away. When Joe Palmer pulled his gun on me, Joe Palmer said, "Don't you boys try to do anything." I never did get my hand on my gun and I never did shoot at Joe Palmer, who shot me.

Witness my hand at Huntsville, Texas, this the 23rd January, 1934.

Joe Palmer :

When Ray and I escaped from Eastham farm, it wasn't necessary for Major Crowson to be killed. But I hated Crowson and I killed him because I hated him. We could have made it without shooting anybody. I killed Crowson because of mistreatment to convicts. Ray didn't shoot him and I am making this statement for the sake of my own conscience. That's the truth, and I'm prepared to die.

Clyde :

it were never part of the plan for Henry Methvin to pile in the car but when I heard Joe Palmer holler through the fog Give us something else I sprayed the air with guard detergent and thats what give them others the idea to come on

one feller what scooted past saw we only had a coupe and he kept running and I never did get his name

Git outta here Jimmy Mullen told Methvin and Bybee This aint a bus but I said Shut the hell up and let em be if they got stones enough to run for it then let em be

they sardined in the rumble seat with Joe who said hed killed Crowson which was the mornings high point Ray Hamilton having dropped the clip to his 45 on the ground like a butterfingered fool

Joe was skinny and mean and before a month passed would help me even a score with Wade McNabb but he had a kind streak too tending the caged monkeys and wolves at the prison and once when an inmate jobbed a bear with a stick Joe beat the man half to death

Ray rode saddle on Jimmy up front swearing up and down he was good for the grand

after that Methvin became our new Deacon except he had a voice so soft that I had to holler at him many a time when we was driving to speak the hell up goddamn it

Methvin was so big and dumb I thought he was the ideal sidekick but he undid us with love for his own sorry life its a weakness of mine but I allus trusted a man with an ugly face and I tell you looking at Henry was a goddamn hurt

well eventually he sang his own song and it had a verse or two about us some hack wrote that our days are numbered

Q. Please state your name?

A. Henry Methvin.

Q. Where is your home?

A. Castor, Louisiana.

Q. How old are you?

A. Twenty-four.

Q. You are the defendant in this case?

A. Yes, sir.

Q. On the morning of April 6, 1934, were you in the company of Clyde Barrow and Bonnie Parker by your own choice?

A. No sir.

Q. Did you, or had you at that time, or prior to that time had any prearranged plan or design to do any particular thing, in company with Bonnie Parker and Clyde Barrow?

A. No sir.

Q. Nothing of the kind?

A. No sir.

Q. Your purpose was to try to get them back down home—

MR. CLARK. Objected to: Leading.

MR. NESBITT. I will withdraw the question.

Q. What was your purpose at that particular time you were with them that morning?

A. Trying to get them back down to Louisiana.

Q. Did you have any other purpose other than that in mind?

A. Well I wanted to turn them over to the officers.

but whose aint

Henry Methvin :

the next parish over is a midwife seen a baby born with gold teeth seen another with two faces pop eyes web toes cloven feet

heard tell of a cow give birth to a calf with a human head thats how they knew the dirt farmer had gigged his stock

a dogs tail will draw lightning

switches bunched on your porch means you been warned

once on the bayou blue knives of flame darted before my eyes and between the trees like a flock of scared birds

I was always meant for something large

them two cared nothing for me but kept me prisoner and fetchit boy

its true I helped nab that trustee running his mouth about having Clyde for a prison wife hell I even dropped the map in the mailbox to the Houston paper showing which well to find him in but when them two threatened my folks with death I put my arms around them at Black Lake thinking one thing

you will defeat your enemies if you kill the first snake of spring

Lee Simmons :

At about nine o'clock on the morning of January 16, 1934, Captain B. B. Monzingo, manager of the Eastham farm, called me at Huntsville with more bad news. There had been a raid on the farm, and a number of prisoners had escaped in an automobile provided by an outsider.

Warden Waid and I left hurriedly for Eastham, some forty miles north of Huntsville. On arrival we found that the raiders had opened up with a machine gun, critically wounding a guard, Major Crowson. During the confusion of the attack, several desperate prisoners had escaped: Raymond Hamilton, Joe Palmer, Henry Methvin, and Hilton Bybee.

This raid was the first of its kind. I figured we had to make an example of some people if we were ever to put a stop to this sort of thing.

I was determined to see Raymond Hamilton and Joe Palmer electrocuted for the slaying of Crowson. And I wanted their accomplice of the machine gun likewise captured and condemned. By this time we were convinced that the man who had wielded the machine gun and engineered the entire escape had been none other than Clyde Barrow.

Barrow was just a convict number to me, one of the anonymous men assigned to Eastham farm, one of those who early in my administration appeared in the records as a victim of self-mutilation. For he had cut off a toe in hopes of being transferred to the Walls.

I lay awake nights until I worked out in my mind what I felt to be a feasible plan. It involved a great deal of detail and would require the fullest confidence to be reposed in me by my superiors. In particular it had to have the fullest assistance of the Governor.

First I requested the prison board to create a new position, Special Investigator for the Texas Prison System. This could be done, under the law, with the approval of the Governor, the chairman of the State Board of Control, and the comptroller of accounts. After I had explained my plan, the board and the other necessary officials granted my request.

I told the board I wanted to hire an experienced and dependable person to put on the trail of Clyde and Bonnie and to stay on it until they were either captured or put out of business. Board members asked me who this person would be, and I answered that I did not yet know but that when I had made up my mind I did not intend that they or anybody else should know who he was.

I had my eye on one or two former Ranger captains. I weighed my choice strictly on the basis of who would be the best man for the job. Barrow was a desperado with no regard for human life, a man who despised the law and hated all peace officers. Whoever stopped Clyde Barrow would do so at the risk of his life. I knew from what Bybee and James Mullin (and, after his capture, Palmer) told me that Barrow had made up his mind never to be taken alive and that Bonnie Parker was determined to go down with Clyde. That was the kind of game we had to hunt; it was my task to find a hunter of the kind to handle it.

My decision was for Frank Hamer.

From The Remington Company Files :

You will find enclosed herewith a reel of motion picture film taken at Mexia one week ago. Captain Frank Hamer of the Texas Rangers, along with several other Rangers, were in an action here against some bootleggers. The lawmen were anticipating a shootout, but the surrender came off peaceably. Discussion then began about sharpshooting and it so happened that Captain Hamer was challenged by a fellow Ranger to a friendly shootout, pistol against rifle. He would use his single action .45 Colt, which he affectionately calls "Old Lucky," and the other man would use the rifle of his choice. I was able to get the parties to agree to be filmed, as you will see. Captain Hamer can be seen shooting twenty-five butter dishes from the air. He did not miss a one. Needless to say, the man with the rifle does not fare as well. I recommend that Remington design and manufacture a rifle commemorating the event. It was surely something, and a testament to show that the Old West has not entirely died away.

Frances Augustus Hamer was born on St. Patrick's Day, 1884, to a blacksmith from West Virginia. When he was six years old, the family moved to San Saba County, Texas, where he attended a country school off and on. San Saba was livestock country, and Hamer grew up among the violence of herdsmen. By his teens he was running down stock thieves, and at sixteen he received his first bullet wound, fired from the gun of a would be assassin. On his sickbed, Hamer overheard the doctor tell his father that he wouldn't survive. After that, he claimed to talk with the "Old Master" every night before falling asleep. At seventeen, despite family expectations that he would become a preacher, Hamer left home to wrangle cattle in the Pecos Valley.

At nineteen he conspired with a fellow cowpoke to rob the bank at San Angelo, but when, rifles in hand, they turned their horses onto the street that led to the bank, the pair encountered their foreman in a moment of either serendipity or sheer dumb luck that, years later, Hamer would claim changed his life, saying, "Had I not gone with the law, I would have gone against it."

Given his height, doorframes routinely swatted off his hat, though he moved with the easy grace of a cowboy and carried his bulk like it was horse muscle. His hat brim shadowed his eyes, the left one of which sat enorbed in a darker pool than the right. The skin on his face was rubbery and so smooth it seemed not so much shaven as hairless. He only felt truly at ease around men who, by their stories and temperaments, showed themselves to be comfortable with death. He was fast for his size and liked to fight, especially when outnumbered. He rarely threw punches, opting instead for the application of his boot toes to his opponents' shin bones. On April 21, 1906, he enlisted as a Texas Ranger and went to work in the Rio Grande borderlands.

By the time Lee Simmons asked him to hire on with the Texas Prison System, Frank Hamer had been snatched from death so many times that he believed himself set apart by divine protection. He'd lived during the transition from horse to car and gladly traded in his cowboy boots and gear for a roomy black business suit, white shirt, and tie, thereafter deriding those who persisted in the western look as "pharmaceutical"—by which he meant drugstore—cowboys. He'd killed nearly fifty men and been shot several times, but he despised the press and was so camera shy and shrouded in the fog of legend that a man named John Sawyer made a living impersonating him in vaudeville shows and on the carnival circuit in California and New Mexico despite standing a foot shorter than Hamer, weighing ninety pounds less, and wearing mustaches. John Sawyer was only arrested when he had the audacity to come to Texas. Hamer held no ill will for Sawyer, however—he understood why a man would want to be him, if only for audiences. Hamer caught the train to San Antonio, befriended Sawyer in jail, and posed with him for a rare portrait.

Hamer :

I guess Gonzaullas and Hickman found the idea of shooting a woman unsavory. McDaniel, too, though he probably paled at the suggestion of an ambush. I put in for the federal job hunting Dillinger, but they wanted an attorney, as if that were a qualification.

When the Eastham raid occurred, I was between Ranger stints and working as a strikebreaker for a Houston oil company. The job hunting Barrow and Parker would mean a monthly pay cut of more than $300, yet I'd be free to do things my way. It was no secret that I had bad blood with the Fergusons, but when Lee Simmons made his request for a man of his choosing, Pa showed that he had the rocks even if Ma did not. It seemed like every agency had taken a shot at Barrow—the feds, the Rangers, and about twenty different police forces—so why shouldn't the Texas Prison System throw its hat in the ring?

What I wanted was time and Lee offered it. I liked that old boy for his straight talk. "No matter how long it takes, I'll back you to the limit," he said at my kitchen table over coffees. "The thing for you to do is put them on the spot, know you are right, and then shoot every son of a bitch in sight."

Some would say this is a particular way of thinking, but it is not. It is not Texas logic or western logic. These were people who broke into National Guard armories and had military machine guns and thousands of rounds of ammunition. People who shot peace officers on sight. No. When you are hunting outlaws who are more dangerous than any criminals in all American history, such logic is rational logic.

I was secretly issued a commission as a state highway patrolman, and on the first day of my assignment, I went to work gathering information from other lawmen and agencies and ordering the pair of firearms necessary for the job: a .35 Remington rifle (serial number 10045) from Jake Petmeckey's store in Austin, along with a "police only" magazine that held twenty rounds; and a Colt .38 Super pistol of blue steel. Dillinger pal Leslie Homer said the new .38

Super would level the field with modern gangsters as it could penetrate any bulletproof vest ever made. I also acquired a Ford V8 sedan of the type Barrow preferred, and, on February 11, climbed behind the wheel and drove to Dallas.

Mr. Henry Ford,
While I still have got breath in my lungs I will tell
you what a dandy car you make. I have drove Fords
exclusively when I could get away with one. For
sustained speed and freedom from trouble the Ford
has got ever other car skinned, and even if my business
hasen't been strickly legal it don't hurt anything to tell
you what a fine car you got in the V8 —
    Yours truly
    Clyde Champion Barrow

Hamer :

A man's ear is distinct as his fingerprint
I've trained myself to know its crenellations
I have detected the drone of an airplane
A full minute before other men
At a no ante poker game I smelled
The scorched flesh from a match, its tip stuck
To the finger of a man who'd failed to notice
My eyes can see a travelling bullet, which looks
Like a bee enveloped in a tiny cloud of heat
I see a shotgun blast as a swarm of gnats
And if you were to study animals like me
You'd see that the criminal's nature is that
Of a coyote glancing over its shoulder

An isolated pullout along a desolate road in the deep woods of Bienville Parish. Four men stand in the gap between the hoods of two cars. A cool morning breeze blows through the oldfield pine.

OLD MAN METHVIN. That aint the only sticking point, sheriff. What we say, what you say, puts my boy at risk.

DEPUTY PRENTISS OAKLEY. Don't forget, he's the one what jumped in Barrow's car down there at Eastham.

METHVIN. That were wrongheaded from the start. Before that prison break, he aint never been in no trouble.

OAKLEY. What do you call putting a six inch smile on a feller in west Texas?

METHVIN. Some fairy picks you up and points a gun and orders you to do this faggoty thing and that, tell me what you would do.

OAKLEY. You make a strong case for not riding with strangers.

METHVIN. You are perched on a high horse, Prentiss.

SHERIFF HENDERSON JORDAN. Gentlemen, what help is this?

JOHN JOYNER. What Mr. Methvin would like to know is, can he trust you with certain information?

JORDAN. Are we talking about what I think we're talking about?

METHVIN. Unless you've got a strange notion otherwise.

OAKLEY. It's no secret who your boy's running with.

JOYNER. That's why we wanted to speak with you, sheriff. That's why Mr. Methvin's worried for his boy.

JORDAN. Who wouldn't be?

JOYNER. Clyde and Bonnie were through this very parish not two days ago. They have brought Henry to see his folks twice now.

OAKLEY. And you set eyes on them?

JOYNER. I didn't, no. We want to talk about what can be done for Henry.

JORDAN. That's what I'm here to talk about.

METHVIN. Kindly hard not to set eyes on a person when you eatin supper with him.

Prentiss Oakley wanders to the roadside and stoops among the broomsedge and bluestem to inspect a plant shaped like a candlestick with thistled orbs in place of flametips. He snaps one off.

JOYNER. You can't expect anything from Mr. Methvin without some kind of guarantee. I'm here to represent his interests as a friend of the Methvin family. We want to know what you can do for his boy, sheriff.

OAKLEY. The bigger question is, what can Henry do for us? The question is whether he'll go through with it.

METHVIN. They'll kill my boy if they catch wind of this, and if not them, then some others what know them. Them two murder at the drop of a hat. They'll murder my family in gross and think nothing on it.

Oakley spins the thistled orb as he holds it.

OAKLEY. But if your boy stays with them, they're going to get him killed sooner or later, is that right?

METHVIN. They said their number's up theirselves.

OAKLEY. That's a mighty tight spot.

METHVIN. Can you blame him if he don't want to run with them? My boy wants to live.

JORDAN. What is it *you* want?

METHVIN. You got to be sworn to absolute secrecy. I got to have your word on that first, sheriff.

JORDAN. You have known me to be an honest man, Ivy. You can count on me to do right by you.

JOYNER. What we want is to broker a full Texas pardon for the boy.

OAKLEY. You're a blind hog hunting acorns in the dark, man. Just which state do you think the sheriff works for?

JORDAN. It seems to me it'd be a sight better if Henry surrendered. If he agreed to serve out his attempted murder time, turning himself in would speak highly.

METHVIN. Sounds pretty, but it won't work. Them two have got people everwhere. They'd as soon have him killed than let him loose. He knows their hideouts and whatall. They'd find a way, I tell you. Hell, it aint my boy the law wants. He aint done nothing compared to the world of what them two have done.

JOYNER. You have to admit, sheriff, it's a drop in the bucket.

JORDAN. Let me talk to some people.

JOYNER. He'll want a pardon from the Texas governor.

METHVIN. Ma says anything's got to be in writing—

JOYNER. *Signed* by the governor.

JORDAN. I think it's only natural to want to help your boy, Ivy, but I'm not convinced that Henry's willing to go through with this. Have you spoken with him about it?

METHVIN. He and Ma had a minute by theirselves. Said he wants out.

JORDAN. We'll need some kind of definite assurance before I can do anything.

METHVIN. They said they'd be back. They didn't say when.

JORDAN. Let me see what I can do.

METHVIN. If we meet again, it's got to be under cover of dark. Can't nobody know about this, sheriff.

Oakley hands the orb to Methvin.

OAKLEY. Now, you take an Indian. He would chew the roots of this plant real good, no matter that it would bring on a powerful stomach hurt. You have to wonder why he would do such a fool thing. I'm going to tell you why. So's he could handle a rattlesnake without him getting struck.

METHVIN. I know what it is.

OAKLEY. Maybe you ought to try it.

Old Man Methvin tosses the thistle aside. The men pair off into the cars and drive away in opposite directions. In the air hangs a curtain of dust.

Sheriff Schmid's office shrank with Hamer in it. Ted Hinton doffed his hat while Bob Alcorn backed up and allowed Schmid to circumnavigate the desk and extend his hand. Hamer wore laced shoes, a black suit bulged by a pistol, and a short brimmed black hat that he didn't bother to remove. He crushed their hands and took a seat. Hamer's manner was silent, cryptic, calm. When he did speak, his words were either too withheld or bellowed as if from across a great distance. Schmid inquired cordially about the drive, but a curt answer made clear the man's loathing for persiflage.

The sheriff nodded for Hinton to close the door, then found his seat and laced his fingers under his chin. He reminded them of the meeting's confidential nature before saying, "Captain Hamer, I am assuming that you have never seen Barrow in person."

Hamer lit a cigaret. "Wouldn't know him from Adam's off ox."

Pleased, Schmid nodded. "You are welcome to any intelligence we have. I have had Deputy Alcorn on Barrow for a year, ever since he killed Officer Davis at the McBride place. Davis was a Fort Worth deputy, you know."

Hamer said, "It's a marvel the number of botched operations this boy inspires."

The sheriff's eyebrows shot up. "Well, sir, that night we had no idea who we were up against. Here we laid a trap for a two bit robber, when in wanders Barrow armed to the teeth. For a time, I will tell you, I wanted Barrow to myself, but I no longer care who does the nabbing. So that is why we have agreed to throw our efforts in with yours."

When Schmid invited his deputies' conversation, they recounted what knowledge they had of Clyde Barrow, detailed their tracking methods, reviewed where the Sowers ambush went wrong (Barrow seemed to suspect something afoot; Schmid's warning shout gave him the jump; they lacked sufficient firepower). They told of other close calls they'd engineered: the night they'd almost sideswiped him with a heavy truck on loan from the Bill Biggs Excavating Company, an operation aborted at the last minute by Schmid; the time near Duncanville when Hinton, driving a borrowed

Cord sedan, spotted Barrow then threw the linkage by shifting too quickly; the afternoon when the deputies were driving another rent car, this a Cadillac limousine, and gave chase out by White Rock Lake, only to watch him roar off.

Hamer smoked as he listened then stubbed out his cigaret. "Is this where someone makes a Keystone Cops joke?" he said and let them squirm in their chairs before asking about Bonnie Parker's gun skills.

They told what they knew—unable to walk without help, usually only drives the getaway car, and the confession claim made by their captured sidekick, William Daniel Jones, that she fired a pistol from the car window on the night Officer Davis was killed.

"It's too bad Bonnie ever got mixed up with old Clyde," Hinton said as a trifle, but the remark caused Hamer to look at Hinton as if a puff of straw had blown out from the man's collar.

"A body didn't know better," Hamer said, "they might say you sounded sweet on Barrow's chippy. I don't believe I've had your credentials, deputy."

Schmid held up a palm. "I knew Ted was a good man and brought him over from the post office when I was elected sheriff. I have known him since he was a boy."

Hinton said, "I've got no sympathies whatsoever for Parker or Barrow either one, but I know their folks. This'll like as not put both their mothers in the grave."

Eyelids nearly sealed shut, Hamer leaned back and nodded, watching the other two, expecting them to see what he had—and if not, then he would've learned something of their makings as well. Finally, he said, "Maybe they gauge things with a different dipstick in the postal service, but I hear tell the Parker girl never takes a bath. Likes to entertain the men one after the other with the gang watching. All except Barrow, who can't get his pencil up no more. Yes, sir. She forces them studs to satisfy her five or six times a day. Mouth is more herpe sore than mouth, and you can imagine what sits between her legs is so chockfull of disease that a sewer rat wouldn't go near it. As far as I'm concerned, Bonnie Parker's just a bitch in heat, and that's how I intend to deal with her."

J. Edgar Hoover :

I'm going to tell the truth about these rats. I'm going to tell the truth about their dirty, filthy, diseased women. I'm going to tell the truth about the miserable politicians who protect them and the slimy, silly, sobsister convict lovers who let them out on sentimental or ill-advised paroles.

Gods dusty
finger a pillar
hessian flies

freckling the sun
thick as a thumb
cutworms mashed

and bleeding
green rabbits
leaping like fleas

over trains
giant derricks
breeding oily

stink and tractor
lights floating
in fields where

rivers run red
with topsoil
I seen a farmer

once touch
a match
to a pile

of rooshan
thistle as big
as a house

the *booomm*
tossed him
rag doll

maybe he put
gasoline
I don't know

but he stood
and laughed
and slapped

his thighs then
fired double
barrels of black

snot and they say
there aint no god
west of Salina

There is no doubt in my mind that many people, particularly those who have lately been in the habit of calling progressive-minded individuals interested in reclaiming the offender "sob-sisters," would contend that locking a man in his cell and doing nothing more, browbeating him, and destroying every vestige of hope constitutes reform. They would probably even infer that we ought to mete out some form of torture occasionally. And all that, of course, would come under the heading of rehabilitation. If some of those people would only become a little less hysterical and read a bit of history they might learn that not only are their theories illogical, but they have never proven effective.

—Lewis Lawes, warden, Sing Sing Prison

8

Stool Pigeons, Spotters, and Rats

May 23rd

It would swallow everything it touches, this tiny mouth, this traveling mouth, this tiny traveling mouth then, the gathered hot breath exhalation of thousands of grains of powder ensorcelled and bound, ancient materials bent to a new purpose and given new names—primer, graphite, nitrocellulose—as if the error were in their original construction and only through recombination could their powers be properly marshaled and set to the task of push, of pushing the mouth across its designated span of openness, bending the grass under its outrageous hunger, the tree branches pulling back at such want, its wide lipped gape shocking the very air to distortion. Things go in the mouth and come out changed, organs swallowed and spat out as grenades, fluid—urine, spinal, blood (Orwell likened being shot by a sniper in the Spanish Civil War to an explosion in the blood)—spewed back into the body as liquid shrapnel, the splintered chips of bones yawing through the tissue of muscles to which they were just attached. And the mouth goes inside things and changes them, cavitating as it goes, opening a channel behind to match the one before. The mouth travels, like us, between twin abysses, and only in stop time, which never really exists because any traveling object—tiny mouth or human body—spinning atop the momentary face of a planet hurtling along an arm of a galaxy itself fragged into cosmic dispersal, is beholden to a formula, $KE = mv^2/2$, that sparked to life with that first bang, and only through such impossibility—that is to say, the force of imagination to freeze the clock—can we know what it's like to ride at the very center of a new holiness.

For the robbery on January 25, 1934, of the Central National Bank in Poteau, Oklahoma, ten days after the prison raid, the gang stole two cars, one as a getaway dummy and the other minded by Bonnie in the woods for the long distance run. When they encountered snow in Missouri, Hilton Bybee splintered from the group, picked up a woman in Vinita, left her in Vega, and was arrested in Amarillo after a fortnight of freedom.

The others stayed together, but tight quarters made for a surly crew. Joe Palmer and Ray Hamilton nursed grudges. During one argument, Joe called Ray "a punk blabbermouth braggart." Later that afternoon, as they rode through the Missouri hills, Ray clicketted the hammer on an army 45 and aimed it at Joe's head while he slept. Henry watched dispassionately to see whether Ray was serious or only playacting, when Clyde, monitoring things in the rearvision, lunged over the seat and backhanded Ray.

The car veered. Clyde spun back around and fought the steering wheel for control, but the front wheels bucked up and over a rise and into the air. Ray hollered, then the whole shebang socked into the ditch.

When they could, they stumbled out, bloody and caked with dust. Under the car hung the telltale vee of a snapped axle. Clyde cursed as he splashed water from a canteen on his face. Then he ordered Ray to hand over his wallet and pistol and thumb it into town to steal a replacement car.

They had bought it on a slow curve with brush on either side. Cold afternoon sunlight lamped the wreck. Joe went back to sleep in the car while they waited. Henry stacked their belongings on level ground, covering the guns with a blanket. Clyde paced the roadside and waved onlookers past, leaning on the sills of the persistently curious to explain away the situation. Meanwhile, Bonnie lounged on the car's running boards, swilling from a flask and chuckling sleepily to herself.

When Henry finished, he gazed down the road toward town, hands on his hips and fingertips in his pockets. Henry was big, half a head taller than Clyde and thick boned. His face wore pock scabs, and a shadow saddled his nose. Bonnie addressed him by one of his nicknames. "Say, Gibbons. If you could be anywhere in the world other than here right now, where would you be?"

"Couldn't say."

"Me, I'd be floating the canals of Venice this very minute, serenaded by a chubby little Italian man. He'd have on suspenders and a big straw hat and sing in this lovely loud voice. I'd have an endless supply of French champagne, and I'd lie back on velvet cushions as we cruised beneath all those white bridges. Everyone would wave and wish they were me."

Henry looked at her as if she were speaking Japanese.

She took a sip then nodded at him with her chin. "I'm a djinnee offering one wish only. Think hard. Paris, Rome, the Nile? A night in New York City? The pyramids of Egypt?"

Henry shrugged.

"Don't act like you've never in your life dreamt of going somewhere exotic."

Henry scratched his head and appeared to suffer true consternation. "It don't do to think much about that sort of thing."

"Just play along, would you? Here I am offering you the whole goddamn globe. It's just a game to pass the time. What'll it be?"

"Truth to tell, I aint so very eager to visit none of them places."

"Haven't you got even a jot of desire to see somewhere spectacular?"

Henry slitted his eyes at the sun, said, "I guess I'd just as soon be home as anywhere," and shot her a goony grin.

"Do you know who I was in Dallas?"

"No, mam."

"A waitress slinging eggs. Wearing a gravy stained apron. Smelling of grease and earning sixty cents a day to get pinched on the ass by no accounts. I was a nobody. No one knew who Bonnie Parker was. I'm telling you I was a loser."

"You like the headlines, then?"

"Hell, no. They're only waving palm leaves."

"Mam?"

"You're just a brush ape hayseed, aren't you." An instant later she turned sympathetic. "I don't mean anything by it. Of course you want to go home and see your folks." She gave a sad smile, then motioned him over and put the dented demijohn in his hand, saying, "Let's be honest. Home is where the whiskey is."

They let Joe Palmer off in Joplin with plans to regroup in a month, then drove south in the car Ray had newly stolen through Muskogee and Hugo, crossing the leaden stretch of the Red River before angling southeast toward Marshall, and, finally, straight east onto the Sabine uplift, where the rolling pine hills were seamed with creeks that swamped out into bayous. Though the country wasn't flat, the greenery crowded so close to the road that it was rare to find any vantage at all. It was only trees and more trees: here, soldiers marching in rows; here, brumal glyphworks; here, the high bunching green of loblolly. Elsewhere, sumac and red buckeye flanked the road. Fresh air. Crows soaring. Glassy ponds lorded over by lonesome gray penitents. By sunset they were deep in back road hallways that were dark and sinister and broken only at times by clearings that might hold a shack unfit for a plumb line or a burn pile coughing slow plumes of smoke.

They had only ever traveled the highways in this region. Once off the cattle trail, Clyde took to the place, proclaimed it an untouched country made for driving. Nightfall reduced the visible world to headlamp beams, when cones of light showed a deer carcass with a twisted neck, a coyote with glowing green eyes, an armadillo on its shellback, the white flicker of a moth before it exploded on the windshield. If he needed to outrun something, he had only to mash the accelerator and the narrow paths, the twisting roads too numerous to map, came faster. Roads led to more roads, each intersection a doubling of dispersion. And though he tried to distrust the notion, he began to feel a sense of safety in the byways of northern Louisiana.

It was in early February, then, that Henry's ploy worked, and they took him to see his parents in Bienville Parish. Ivy and Avie were country folks. He was short and farmer lean, with slung jowls and a frown that looked like it'd been stapled there. Silver hair that tended to white on top, a dark lower half of his face where the shadow of his straw hat stopped, and hands cracked from work but surprisingly supple. He had a habit of putting a pinky finger in his ear, wiggling it, and inspecting the results. He believed his son Henry to be a victim of bad luck. In 1930, when Henry was nineteen and gone to work in the west Texas oil fields, a fellow roughneck offered him a ride, a man in his fifties. The older man drove them into the country, then leaned over and clenched Henry by the throat and made what the youth later described as "strange advances." Henry had a double bladed knife with him, which he used to slit the man's throat, though he failed to kill him. The Texas jury, rather more persuaded by the man's story—that Henry had tried to steal his car—convicted the reticent youth of attempted murder and sentenced him to twelve years. A month ago, hitchhiking and bussing and sleeping in ditches, Ivy traveled the four hundred miles to Austin to deliver papers that, he was convinced, would win his son a pardon. After handing them over, he was told that Clyde Barrow had gotten to his boy first.

Avie was a bitty woman with round eyeglasses that pooled the light on her cheeks. She had a squarish jaw and a grim look. The part down the centerline of her skull gleamed white inside two shells of dark hair. Under a kitchen window studded with frost flowers, she fixed the outlaws cabbage stew, and, with the backs of spoons, they mashed baked beans onto skillet cornbread and let Ray, never short of words, do most of the talking. And though the Methvins invited them to stay at their meager farmhouse, Clyde drove them into the woods, where they made a cold camp and slept in the shed of the car.

In February, they returned to Texas, and it was during this time that Ray took as a girlfriend a woman named Mary O'Dare, the wife of his former partner, Gene O'Dare, with whom he'd been arrested in 1932 while ice skating up in Michigan. On February 18, she accompanied Ray to a twilight meeting with the Barrow and Parker families on the Dallas outskirts, where everyone sat around a wafting picnic basket and tried not to think about the fried chicken inside while they waited for the kids. A car approached and flashed its lights, then Bonnie could be seen in the front seat, clapping and waving, with Clyde driving, and the golem of Henry in back.

Clyde and Bonnie gave several hundred dollars to the families and related the particulars of the three January bank robberies that had netted the gang $5,600 in eight days. Bonnie arranged with Emma to buy her a new dress. "Something green," she said, "with a slim waist and a belt like all the girls are wearing now."

Mary eagerly inserted herself, though knowing only Ray. She was stout and curvy, with blue eyes that offset her brown hair, cream puff cheeks, a button chin, and gapped incisors. She was smitten with romantic notions of the criminal life, yet the presence of Bonnie and Clyde themselves had little effect on her other than inciting her to explain how everything, somehow, related to her. Within minutes the group knew her pet peeves (work, snuff, dogs, and facial hair) and weaknesses (men and money), that she was the victim of two failed marriages despite being only nineteen, and that she prided herself on refusing pity. She drew lines of minute distinction around ways of acting and thinking so grounded in the stuff of Hollywood that a generous judge of her character might label it merely idiosyncratic.

On the ride home, Cumie looked like she was chewing a lemon. She told Emma, "Next time I see that woman coming, I'm taking to the tall timber."

Nevertheless, when Bonnie and Clyde again teamed with Ray, Mary rode along. On February 27, they robbed the R. P. Henry and Sons Bank in Lancaster, Texas, then fled north, toward Indiana. Along the way, the men bought matching tailored suits and mercerized

Pepperell shirts and overcoats with storm straps on the sleeves. They found a deserted place outside of a small town, stood atop the foundation wall of a vanished structure, and made pictures.

One of the shots shows Clyde cupping Ray's clenched fist, an image that suggests Clyde and Ray were lovers. That could be. It could also be that it was simply an act of solidarity in a time when displays of male affection were less sexually suggestive: here are two West Dallas boys who came from the same streets, decked out in gangster suits and shiny fedoras, looking into the world's eyes with go to hell stares. Who's to say what feelings stir from those held hands?

What's known for certain is that Mary incited troubles within the group. Bonnie disliked her from the start, claimed she could fry flapjacks with all the makeup on her face, and found her so common that she called her "the washerwoman" behind her back. Time and again while they were on the road, Mary wanted to go off to town alone, but Bonnie wouldn't let her out of her sight for fear she was plotting to turn them in.

On the drive to Terre Haute, arguments broke out over the division of the Lancaster loot. Clyde and Bonnie got into a scrap, but the crew pressed on. That night, while camped, Mary sidled up to a sulking Bonnie and suggested poisoning Clyde with knockout drops, then forming a new gang. She opened her purse to reveal, within a jumbled mix of combs, tweezers, mirrors, and powder pouches, a small brown prescription bottle. Bonnie, of course, shared this news with Clyde, who gave Ray an ultimatum: leave behind either Mary or the gang.

The next day, Ray stole a car and drove with Mary back to Texas. It would be a little more than a year later, on April 5, 1935, when Ray was arrested for the last time and asked by Dallas reporters about Mary O'Dare, that he said, "That girl ratted on me to save her own neck." A month later, he was tied to the electric chair at Huntsville with eight leather harnesses. When the warden asked if he had anything to say, Ray replied, "Yes sir. The governor's office has asked me for information about the Hillsboro murder. I didn't do that job. The man who killed Bucher is dead now, but even if he wasn't, I wouldn't tell you people anything about it." (He was, of course, referring to Ted Rogers, whom he resembled.) After exchanging pleasantries with the priest in the room, Ray had his forehead and chin cinched to the chair back with more leather straps. The restraints pulled the motive force from his face and gave him a vapid, inhuman aspect. The top of his head had been shaved clean, and a sea sponge soaked in brine was placed there under the brass headpiece. Where his trousers leg had been slit, copper electrodes shaped like stars were attached to his left calf. The priest made the sign of the cross before Ray's fishlike eyes, then a leather mask was dropped over his face.

Mary O'Dare :

What got me was how dirty them two kept themselves.
The car reeked with their sour smell. They had dirty
hair, dirty clothes, and they didn't seem to care. Matter
of fact, they preferred it that way. One time when Ray
and I was with them, we made them stop beside a creek
that was iced over. Ray took a stone and broke a hole
in the ice so we could wash our faces and brush our
teeth. I looked up at Bonnie and Clyde sitting in that
warm car and they was just laughing at us like there
was no tomorrow.

Bonnie and Clyde and Henry met up again with Joe Palmer, who'd paid a Houston attorney to have the Eastham building trustee Wade McNabb released on his own recognizance, a common practice of the time known as buying furlough that was allowed to a prisoner who'd accepted a position of authority and, over time, earned the warden's trust. Then the crew drove to the east Texas town of Gladewater and trolled its streets and dropped questions and, late one night, located McNabb in a domino parlor.

From Dallas, Hamer took to the road, driving the Arklatex triangle, with loops into Missouri and Oklahoma as necessary. At one point he tracked his prey to North Carolina, where they had toured a cigaret factory. Years later, he would tell Walter Prescott Webb, the only biographer he ever allowed close, that he was trying to discover the "mental habits" of his prey: "When I began to understand Clyde Barrow's mind, I felt that I was making progress. I learned that Barrow never holed up at one place; he was always on the go; and he traveled farther in one day than any fugitive that I have ever followed. He thought nothing of driving a thousand miles at a stretch."

Hamer ate on the go, quick bites from sandwich stands, plates carried out from restaurants. Sometimes, he bought a loaf of sliced bread and folded one piece after another into his mouth as he drove. He drank coffee from a Stanley vacuum bottle stored under the seat and suffered a knotted neck sleeping wedged into the car along dirt roads. Wakened by a window tap early one morning, he showed his badge to a highway patrolman who stammered an apology when he read the name on it.

In the third week of February, he began sleeping in hotels. He called his wife when he could. Every two weeks, he sent Lee Simmons a "Traveling Expense Account" sheet, noting where he stayed for $1.75 or $2.00 per night, and each meal taken, a thirty five cent breakfast at the Liberty Coffee Shop, a forty five cent dinner at the City Cafe.

What he relished most were details, tidbits that rendered his quarry less newsprint phantom, more flesh and bone. From interviews and photographs, he built mental images of what they looked like. He educated himself on their preferred cigarets, food, and clothing. No one had hunted them like this, and he had a great advantage: they didn't know he was tracking them. He came across their trail in Texarkana, found where they'd purchased a half gallon of whiskey in Logansport, discovered that they bought gasoline near Keechi, then, according to his log, "went in the night to a negro house and had the negroes cook them some cornbread and fry a chicken."

Less than a month into Hamer's work, the Division of Investigation, who'd been tracking the Barrow gang for thirteen months at the time, was alerted to his assignment. Special Agent Frank Blake, in charge of the Dallas office, wrote a memo to J. Edgar Hoover on March 17, stating that "he is working in close harmony with us" and that "he is an officer with whom agents of the Division can work with fullest confidence"—and in this, Hamer gained another great advantage.

On the same day, Agent E. J. Dowd filed another memo detailing his work conducted with Hamer over the previous ten days. Information extracted from Hilton Bybee led them to a Barrow hideout on a hilly strip of land outside of Wichita Falls. There, along the Wichita River, Hamer insisted on walking the grounds solo. He would stoop to touch something or stand stock still while jotting in a small notebook. When he came across tire tracks, he unspooled a cloth measuring tape and found the vehicle to have a one hundred six inch wheelbase. The tracks led to the remnants of a campsite. In the fender of an abandoned Ford that'd been used for target practice, he fitted his fingertips to bullet holes. He examined shards of shattered bottles and riddled cans of Vienna sausage. He touched the flattened grass where three people had bedded down under blankets, he rolled cigaret castoffs between his thumb and forefinger (Camels with lipstick stains, Bull Durhams without), he held discarded bread crusts, he slipped a coat button into his pocket. And when he toed apart the campfire ashes, there lay a wad of blackened receipts, one of which was still legible. It recorded a dress purchase from Lord's at 1510 Elm Street in Dallas.

Dowd and Hamer made the trip to the store, where a saleslady named Miss Yantis retrieved a style 596 dress from the display rack and modeled it for the officers. Green rabbit wool with an ascot tie. White fringe down the front, green fringe down the sleeves. A belt of matching material, one and a half inches wide with a nickel plated buckle.

The Execution of Wade McNabb

Everywhere death. Road death. Gun death. Middle of the night death. Get on your knees and pray.

Do it quick do it now

I will kill thy root with famine, and he shall slay thy remnant. Howl, O gate. Cry, O city.

There shall come from the north a smoke. A frenzied hum and clank shall roll over the land. Behold, the Lord shall come with fire in the last days, and with his chariots like a whirlwind, to render his anger with fury, and his rebuke with flames of fire.

He stepped through the door and went up to the only person in the place, an old man sitting at a desk. He leveled the shotgun and said politely, I don't want to hurt you, but I've got to have your money.

The old man grinned. Son, I wish you would put that gun up and stop being funny. This bank's been closed for four days. There aint a dollar bill in it. Look around, the place is a dustbin.

He left laughing so hard his stomach ached.

They walk him farther down

And farther still

The well is around here somewheres

Just a board on the ground

Lift its edge

Peer in and down

Piney woods and rolling hills, rivers and streams, pecan trees and grapevines. East Texas was beautiful country once. Whippoorwills would sing to the stars behind the stars at night.

Dad Joiner had a dream just before he was about to commit suicide down in Galveston. Fell asleep on the seawall and saw a gentle sloping pasture bordered by a stream.

Used to be, you'd strip and swim across the river on your back, clothes held above the water. Now, waterways are thick with oil waste. Pastures are truck rut, roads axle high rivers of red sludge.

Old Dad hurried to his car and made a pencil sketch of his dream. He'd seen the place before, he just knew. When he found it, he carried a Bible into the homes of widows and quoted from it with his eyes closed and sold future shares then drove down the road and sold those same shares again.

Had to drill that sucker three times before it popped. Roughnecks and whores and hot oil. Daisy Bradford number three: Floodgates.

What kind of fool would plant an orchard when mineral rights are the future?

Lights in every direction. A forest of derricks topped with flare stacks. After dark, kids play baseball by these flames of fire.

Move him to the edge

What you need to do is get on your knees and pray

Billy the Kid never had such a chance as you

Hold this

Are you praying

Do it now

Do it quick

There thats done

Goddamn it

Pop him again hes still moving

The boy done rolled him in

Wait for the splash just wait

Nothing then more nothing

Maybe he fell to China the boy says

Peer in and down

The earth opens here

The opposite of light

The opposite of somewheres

Rocks dropped in the same thing

Where do they go

They go to the opposite of somewheres

Where they go there are no maps

Why is this other place so perfect?

Untouched streams. Rolling hill country. Boggy quiet.

Near Chandler's Camp above Campti, there was a family having a fish fry who invited them over. Fed them fried perch, fresh caught, until they thought they would burst. She carved her initials into a 25 automatic, then gave it to the mother in the morning.

There's oak, hickory, pine, persimmon, red cedar, black gum, sweet shrub. Crows flying low over the treetops. The Lord saw fit to seed northern Louisiana with passion vine and possum haw, flowering spurge and wild ginger, milkweed and pussytoes.

Solomon's seal. Wild bergamot.

Yellow stargrass that looks nothing like flame tips.

Let's us move our families here.

All my love.

Mapless. Random and shining. Without a whit for the tattered world.

They spread a blanket under a walnut tree. She was holding a cucumber and a paring knife when he said, Look up, hon.

There between branches, a mass of white stars swept past in the wind. As far as the eye could see, separate streams hundreds of feet up, the higher currents slower than the nearer ones. Cottonwood seeds.

She's floating on a river on a raft, the current carrying her swiftly along in the dark. She has no oar, the raft no rudder, no sail. It's just her, floating under a road of stars.

She opens her eyes. Across window dark a star burns a wound in the sky.

They're in the car, her hair taken down and brushing his cheek. Then she's tugging his sleeve, but he's long gone, and it's just her, hugging his ribs, holding on to his heat.

It's dark. She's floating on a river on a raft.

The white man has taken the country we loved and we

only wish to wander the prairie until we die.
(Ten Bears)

Jefferson thought it would take a hundred generations to settle the uninhabitable southern part of the Louisiana Purchase, which he called the blank spot on the map.

Love everywhere. Car love. Gun love. Middle of the night love. Give thanks and drive.

A convicted felon, whom the law in its humanity punishes by confinement in the penitentiary instead of with death, is subject while undergoing that punishment, to all the laws which the Legislature in its wisdom may enact for the government of that institution and the control of its inmates. He has, as a consequence of his crime, not only forfeited his liberty, but all his personal rights except those which the law in its humanity accords to him. He is for the time being the slave of the State. He is *civiliter mortuus*; and his estate, if he has any, is administered like that of a dead man.

—Ruffin v. The Commonwealth, 1871

9

KILLERS

May 23rd : Ted Hinton

Clyde has pulled even with the engine part of the parked truck, twenty feet in front of me, and he is in my gunsight, though his car is still moving. Suddenly, Alcorn's deep bellow "HALT!" arouses him. Alongside him Bonnie screams, and I fire and everyone fires, and in the awful hell and noise Clyde is reaching for a weapon, and the wheels are digging into the gravel as he makes a start to get away. My BAR spits out twenty shots in an instant, and a drumbeat of shells knifes through the steel body of the car, and glass is shattering.

For a fleeting instant, the car seems to melt and hang in a kind of eerie and animated suspension, trying to move forward, spitting gravel at the wheels, but unable to break through the shield of withering fire.

I see a weapon go up; Clyde's head has popped backward, his face twisted at the shock of pain as the bullets strike home. No shots are firing from inside the car, but I do not notice.

Now my shotgun is in my hand; the tan car seems to rock as it absorbs the blasts, but the car is moving forward, it is thirty feet away, thirty-five, it is getting away—

Dramatis Demortuos

Inmate, brother of twelve.

Store owner, husband, father. Optician.

Husband, father of three young children, undersheriff.

Salesman, husband, father, son.

Deputy sheriff. *A martyr to his duty* carved on his stone.

Constable, farmer, husband, father of two girls, one boy. Forty one.

The Irishman. Widower, fiancé, detective.Someone call my mother. She's eighty one.

Failing farmer. Marshal for a month. Hung on for three days.

Eastham woods native, highrider, former barber. Twenty four. Hung on for ten days.

Brother, son. Face down, arms crossed, praying.

Husband, patrolman. Over breakfast agreed with his wife the dead are too soon forgotten.

First day as a patrolman. Fiancée wore her wedding dress to his funeral.

Contractor, Oklahoman. Single father of four. Constable for fifteen dollars a week.

The Easter Killings

The southern plains are moody. Caliche outcrops and stony knobs and warped shelves wend across hardpan. Baked canyons drop away sudden and mysterious. The animals stand as deformed effigies of themselves, waiting to be snuffed out by the droughts and blizzards, grass fires and hailstorms, flash floods and tornadoes and freeze ups. It took a million years of glacial storms to create the loess richness but only ten to destroy, and *on Easter morn, it came to pass that a Ford sedan drove through the plains and was come to a country offshoot outside the city of Grapevine. And, behold, out stepped a man with a machine gun and a woman with a sawed off shotgun, and they did take target practice on a board they laid against a barbed wire fence. And as Methvin, their companion, did keep watch, this man with the machine gun lifted the dress of the woman with the sawed off shotgun and they made open love against the turtleback under the sun. Now a pair of motorcycle officers passed and beheld the sight, and they gathered and neared so that they might speak to them. And as the officers did rack their cycles and turn to salute them, this man with the machine gun and this woman with the sawed off shotgun did raise their guns and smite them. And when the woman with the sawed off shotgun did see that one of the officers yet lived, she stood over him and listened to him plead for his life and watched him wave his hands before his face. Then she slew him. And the woman said to her companions, Behold his head how it did bounce! And with their lust thus slaked, the three made haste and straightway departed thence.*

While Clyde drove, Bonnie perused the paper.
He glanced over when he saw her stiffen.
On the front page was their latest caper.
She sat up, cried out, said, *Wudya listen . . .*

> Tooth prints on a cigar stub led authorities today to attribute the slaying of two Texas highway patrolmen to Clyde Barrow, notorious Southwest killer, and his woman companion, Bonnie Parker.
>
> The officers, E. B. Wheeler, 26 years old, and H. D. Murphy, 28, were shot down without warning late yesterday when they dismounted from their motorcycles to question a man and a woman seated in a parked motor car near Grapevine. Witnesses said neither officer had a chance to draw his weapon.
>
> A. C. Howerton, Fort Worth detective, said he was convinced the slayers were Barrow and the Parker woman. Near the scene of the shooting he said he found a cigar butt bearing the imprint of small teeth. Bonnie Parker's liking for big black cigars is well known.

Can that buncombe! Big black cigars, my ass!
The newspapers print only what aint true.
A stogie will turn me as green as grass.
Who pays these stooges to write what they do?

Austin, Texas, June 6—Hamer and his wife and two children live in a beautiful bungalow framed with cedar trees on Riverside Drive. A woman neighbor was telling me how Hamer loved her cat and was fond of all animal pets. After he returned from Louisiana, he was on her porch petting her cat and she said to him:

"Captain Hamer, I wonder how you can have the heart to kill people when you have such a kind heart toward dumb animals. Aren't you ever sorry for having to kill people that way?"

"I never had the slightest regret. I never killed anyone except human vermin that deserved killing," was the answer.

I asked Hamer if he had any regrets in killing the woman, Bonnie Parker.

"I hated to have to shoot her," he replied. "But, as they drove up that day and I pulled down on Barrow, knowing that some of my rifle bullets were going to snuff out her life along with his, I recalled how she had helped Barrow kill nine peace officers. There ran through my mind, in an instant, how she and Barrow had killed a highway patrolman on Easter Sunday and, after he was lying in the road, dead, she walked over to him, turned him over with the toe of her shoe as he laid face up, and fired another bullet through his body that penetrated the ground a foot. That was done in wanton cruelty, because she knew the man was already dead. Thinking of that as I drew down on them and sighted down my rifle barrel, I gritted my teeth and pulled the trigger as quickly as I could—pulled it again and again.

"If you are an officer sworn to do your duty, you can't afford to feel mercy for such murdering rats, whether they are male or female."

"How many gun fights with criminals have you been in?" I asked.

"I don't mind telling you that. I have been in fifty-two of them, counting the scrimmages we had with Mexicans and smugglers along the Rio Grande," he said.

"How many times have you been shot?"

"Well, I don't mind telling you that. I have been wounded by bullets twenty-three times. Several of those bullets are in me yet. I'd rather have them in than to go through the trouble of having them cut out."

"I hear that you have a great many enemies, some of whom have hired men to kill you."

"That is true. I have been ambushed four different times and shot down, left for dead, twice. I was on crutches for almost a year from wounds given me by men who were paid to kill me."

"Did you ever find out who they were?"

"I did."

"And you had them arrested, I suppose?"

He gave a sort of grunt through his nose, and with a shrug of his shoulders, shook the ashes slowly from his cigaret and said, "No, they were never arrested."

In late April, Bienville Parish Sheriff Henderson Jordan met the Texans. Referred to him by Caddo Parish Sheriff Tom Hughes, Hamer and Alcorn sat in Jordan's Arcadia office and listened to him detail what he knew about Clyde Barrow and Bonnie Parker.

Jordan wore a brown suit on his small shouldered frame. His wide set eyes sunk into a broad face. Parenthetical creases around his mouth suggested a perpetual frown, and his ruddy skin gave him a windblown aspect. He thought and moved slowly and considered himself the unremarkable sheriff of a quiet parish until March 24, 1934, when Agent Lester Kindell of the Division of Investigation and Deputy Sheriff Steve Norris of neighboring Bossier Parish paid him a quarter hour visit, explaining that Ivy Methvin, the father of Bonnie and Clyde's sidekick, Henry Methvin, had moved somewhere north of Coushatta, which put him in Bienville Parish, though just barely.

Like most sheriffs in a nine state region, Sheriff Jordan had followed the Barrow gang exploits and tried to imagine his course of action were they to appear within his jurisdiction. When that reality materialized, Jordan spent ten days traveling his parish's southwestern corner, discreetly inquiring from cotton farmers about new neighbors. What he found led him to believe that the killers were using the Ivy Methvin farm as an infrequent stopover.

"What is it you know, sheriff?" Hamer said.

Jordan took in the lawmen before him, Hamer with his hooded, certain eyes that had seen so much if the stories were to be believed and Alcorn with his canny smile. The Easter killings had led L. G. Phares, head of the Texas Highway Patrol, to offer all his organization's resources, and the Cal Campbell killing in Oklahoma on April 6 spurred US Attorney General Homer Cummings to order the Department of Justice to use all means necessary to capture the killers.

Sheriff Jordan said that a local man named John Joyner was his informant close to the Methvin family; that the Methvin farm, a rent place, was located down an overgrown two track in deep woods crisscrossed with other narrow roads that made for an easy escape;

that the killers visited about every two weeks, usually after dark, when a car would race into the homestead, then dash away about an hour later—just long enough, he surmised, for Henry to see his folks; and that a raid coordinated on April 13, combining heavily armed federal officers with lawmen from two parishes, was called off when Barrow changed his stated plans.

After some time of close questioning, Alcorn nodded. "I believe your information is the best we've had so far."

Hamer agreed, and added, "All the bushes are being shaken for these two. Underworld contacts in every city within a thousand miles have been squeezed. I've been on Barrow nigh on ten weeks and have covered fifteen thousand miles learning his movements. I've documented nine murders, more than a dozen holdups, and untold other petty thefts these two have committed. During it all, I've built a weather map of their movements. What they have are the instincts of wild horses. I am convinced that, given time, they will return to their home range. We have only to set a steel trap. I believe we can do it here."

The lawmen talked until the windows grew dark. Jordan suggested driving his parish's southwestern roads together to familiarize themselves with the territory, and in this way, the partnership that would spell death for Bonnie and Clyde was brokered. Each man would bring a second—for Alcorn, it would be Dallas Deputy Ted Hinton, who, like Alcorn, knew Barrow and Parker on sight; for Hamer, former Texas Ranger Manny Gault; and for Jordan, Deputy Prentiss Oakley who, when the time came, would fire the shot that killed Clyde Barrow.

Clyde :

one day when I was still in school a boy called me po buckra now I have always protected our name so I fought him and he bloodied my face and knocked me down so I got a board and waited and as I waited I prayed that he would come along and when he did I about busted that niggers skull open

that first time they held me down I could see the sun through the trees and hear the locusts sawing away heres something to write home about the guard said Crying Tom they called him because hed laugh and weep at the same time and he clocked me in the face with his pistol and all I could think about was putting a bullet in him so I prayed for that chance though it never came

as for the one they called Big Ed well many a time I prayed for his path to be made slippery as it says in the psalms and one night he came for me in the showers and I watched his eyes jelly as that pipe broke his brain and thats how my first killing like all them that followed were an answer to prayer and the prayer is just this let me alone

On May 4, 1934, Agent interviewed RAYMOND HAMILTON at the County Jail in Dallas, and Raymond stated that if he ever had an opportunity, he would kill Clyde Barrow; that he, of course, knows how Barrow could be contacted but he would not divulge this information to any officer—even to save himself from the electric chair; that after he and Clyde separated at Terre Haute, Indiana, he met Clyde on the highway about a week before Easter Sunday, April 1, 1934, at a lunch stand at Decatur, Texas; that Clyde asked him at that time when they were going to join up again and he told Clyde that they were never going to join again.

—Special Agent C. B. Winstead

They had slept in their clothes in the car in a low stand of birch surrounded by pine. With the windows open, they could hear but not see the creek beyond the dark row of pines. When Clyde woke, the interior was swimming with white smoke, the spirits of fish who'd swum the bygone waters of this spot.

Bonnie was staring at him, smoking a cigaret. "Help me to the creek," she said.

Clyde called to Henry, who was lying on a blanket outside.

"What is it?"

"Carry Sis to the creek."

Bonnie shot Clyde a look but said nothing. When Henry appeared in the window, he rubbed his eyes with his fingers and stretched, then opened the door.

She leaned on his shoulder, hopping on her good leg until they reached the pines, then he bent and scooped her up. She hooked an arm over his neck and held on. At the water's edge, Henry lowered her so that she could sit on a stump. When she made a motion, he undid the latch on her dress. She peeled down the top to reveal a silk undergarment, then caught his eye and said, "Go on now. Let me have my bath."

"I'll be at the car," Henry said, but the walk and the effort had wakened him, and as he passed an oak, it was youthful devilry that caused him to step behind its trunk as a joke. He poked out his head, expecting her to scold him, but she'd already dropped her dress into a pile. He started to holler, but something stopped him.

She took her undergarment by its bottom hem and unpeeled it up and over her and let it fall on her dress. Her breasts surprised him with their fullness despite her skeleton frame. Then she stood and steadied herself with a hand on the stump and slid off her underwear. The way she moved, her joints still liquid with youth, contained also hitches of pain, stops and starts. Was she twenty five, thirty, an ancient forty?

She stepped gingerly down the bank into the creek, her buttocks and the backs of her legs flat and glowing whiter than cotton. Her spine knuckled out from under the skin. She eased further down, then, as she turned, he glimpsed, just before they submerged, a tattoo high up on her right thigh, a dark shock of pubic hair, and the small hill of her stomach with its twinned scars.

Then she looked right at him.

He ducked behind the oak. His heart bucked. Tree bark pressed designs into his palms. A dun spider moseyed past an inch from his nose. His breath was the only thing he heard.

Bonnie :

This close
hes a blue
blur, eye

a spider under
a ledge, breath
a soft wind

He could be
a fevered boy,
milk sick

or a thick lipped
banker, chin slick
with grease

Seen die did I
a little girl
in the face

of a crone,
bobbing up
from silver

depths. Now
the moon
sliding into us

say something
why should I
go to hell
you first

is it ten oclock
I guess it is in Boston

he was in the cafe
why aint he come out
its fate you know
what did fate ever do for me

its quiet out there
too quiet
your feet feel like horn
oh shut up

is it morning yet
I guess it is in Boston

you are a good person
Im a bag of meat
take these off
put your hand right here

Emma Parker :

We saw them for the last time on Sunday evening, May 6. They had chosen a spot four miles east of Dallas. We went out and were with them about two hours, I guess. I sat on the ground under the stars and talked to Bonnie for a long time that night. I remember that as she talked, she was showing me some new snapshots she and Clyde had taken.

"Mama," she began, with that peculiar calm which she and Clyde were always in when speaking of death, "when they kill us, don't let them take me to an undertaking parlor, will you? Bring me home."

I reached out and seized her wrist. "Don't, Bonnie, for God's sake!" I cried. I wanted to scream.

There she sat, so young, so lovely—only twenty-three—with the May moonlight sifting through her yellow hair and making shadows on her cheeks—there she sat and talked to me of death as calmly as if she were discussing going to the grocery store. Bonnie looked up at me and smiled. It was a funny smile—as if she were a million years older.

"Now, Mama, don't get upset," she said to me. "It's coming—you know it—I know it—all of Texas knows it. So don't let them keep me at the undertakers. Bring me home when I die—it's been so long since I was home. I want to lie in the front room with you and Billie and Buster sitting beside me. A long, cool, peaceful night together before I leave you. That will be nice—and restful." She turned one of the pictures toward me. "I like this one," she went on calmly. It was a picture of Clyde holding her up in his arms. They were both laughing. Bonnie's red lacquered fingers caressed the surface of the picture slowly. "And another thing, Mama," she went on, "when they kill us, don't ever say anything—ugly—about Clyde. Please promise me that, too."

I promised her, and I kept my promise where Clyde was concerned, but the people of Dallas would not let me keep the other one. Bonnie never came home when she died, because I could not bring her through the crowds. My little street was black with people that night and it took a cordon of police for me to get through.

Clyde :

at home I met daddy graveside with papers for my
coffin money

said I been a burden on you and mama and all for who
I am

were your folks daddy said and you our boy

but I wanted things accounted for and he witnessed
my penwork

then I took a pebble from Bucksters grave and put
it in my pocket and walked on down the bank to the
boulevard in twilight

east what was east

wouldnt you know it the awful scrimmed edges of
downtown and them glass lights

so this is where my flesh will end my bones under sun
after setting sun nights filled with the citys hum and
the traffic going past and the pouring rain

okay okay

knowing the Lord will pull from the ashes only them as
walk into the fire

Bonnie :

The road gets dimmer and dimmer;
Sometimes you can hardly see;
But it's fight, man to man,
And do all you can,
For we know we can never be free.

We don't think we're too smart or desperate,
We know that the law always wins;
We've been shot at before,
But we do not ignore
That death is the wages of sin.

Some day we'll go down together;
They'll bury us side by side;
To few it'll be grief—
To the law a relief—
But it's death for Bonnie and Clyde.

Henderson Jordan :

The doggerel elegy written by Bonnie Parker had been given to a Dallas newspaper with the understanding that it would not be published before her death. Bonnie Parker's desire to be buried beside Clyde Barrow was denied. Their graves, in different cemeteries, are miles apart.

Hamer :

Regarding our conversation by phone, the gang appeared at Terrell Methvins house on the night of Tuesday, May 9, about eight p.m. Terrell and family were at church. They left and went to Old Man Methvins house about four miles distant which is situated on the edge of the Black Lake swamp, 101 miles south of Shreveport.

The old man lives on a dead road which is rough and in places boggy. On the way to the old mans place Clyde ran over a pole which broke and tore up his battery. They taken a battery out of the old mans truck. They then went to Terrells house arriving about eleven at night and went inside and slept until three a.m. and Old Man M woke them up.

They are driving a V8 black four door sedan. They told Old Man M they would see him soon. They were in Dallas last Saturday night, the fifth, trying to contact the old lady but Joe Bill Francis had taken her and Billie to Nacogdoches. Their intentions are to get Billie for Henry. If the trap here fails I know what their plans are and I will keep you posted.

Bonnie as I told you before is in a delicate condition.

They're out there somewhere right now, Frank Hamer thought a fortnight before he helped execute them. *They're doing something at this instant because they're alive, and every living creature takes up space and moves and eats, and right now, they're sleeping or driving or eating. Maybe they're doing all three this very minute. Maybe the Parker girl's passed out in the passenger seat and Barrow's driving while he eats a slice of ham folded inside a piece of bread. It's dark and they're on a back road somewhere in the deep woods not far from here, though they may as well be driving the craters of the moon, there are so many godforsaken pig tracks in this backwoods country. But maybe Barrow's the one talking. He's talking to Methvin, who's riding in the back. And in the back, it's dark, and in that darkness, Methvin touches the 45 Barrow has given him. He runs his fingers along the smooth steel barrel, and he traces with a fingertip the diamond patterns on the walnut handle, and he looks at the dark knob of Barrow's head, where it's silhouetted by the glow out the front window, dipping every so often to take another bite, and he thinks,* ratchet, aim, squeeze, squeeze, squeeze, *then,* aim again, *this time at the girl, and* squeeze, squeeze, squeeze. *Do it,* Hamer thinks, *do it you limp dicked cretin. Quick, before you think too much on it.* But what if Barrow gave him an empty gun. What if this is a test. What if he can read his mind. *See, there you go. You're not going to do it, are you. You are a weak hearted son of a bitch. Like a rabbit that dies, untouched, of fright,* Hamer thinks. *This is why you can never be me.*

The whole plan is necessarily rather indefinite due to the fact that Barrow never lets anyone know definitely what his plans might be, and the Methvins can never be sure when and how he will arrive or how long he will remain. It appears that any definite plans concerning the details of the raid will have to be worked out on the spur of the moment and after information has been received from the Methvins regarding Barrow's arrival in the vicinity of their homes in Bienville Parish. Due to the inaccessibility of the section in which the Methvins live, and the necessity for the utmost secrecy in this matter, it appears that the success of the plan will have to depend upon a small group of officers working quietly and quickly.

—Special Agent R. Whitley

May 9th, 1934

what werent
nailed down
rose blooming
and blew east

turned out
Chicagos lights
buried New York Citys
streets where people

got a gift from us
four pounds
each of good
southern dust

Letter received by the *Houston Press* :

I could go on for hours reciting cases of inhuman treatment that have been meted out to the unfortunates of the Texas prison system at the hands of Wade McNabb and other building tenders. It is an inhuman slaughter inside those places. We are contributing our bit by sending you a map which will lead to the carcass of one of Lee Simmons's chief rats.

10

DEATH ON RINGGOLD ROAD

May 23rd

They kept our graves apart
though Dallas to us both was home.
Now Ringgold's the place
we go for grace,
alone together, together alone.

Henderson Jordan :

At last we found what seemed to be a perfect spot. It was about three miles north of Sailes and situated on a north-and-south stretch of highway. The road swung down a fairly sharp grade, over a small rise, and then to a steeper hill. The place for our ambush was on the rise. The road cut through the small hill to leave an embankment of about three feet in height on both sides.

In throwing back the earth from the cut, the highway workers had created a low ridge along the east embankment. Grass and weeds along the edge made a perfect cover. The forest receded and the sides of the road were lined with trees and brush.

Prentiss Oakley :

In the crotches of trees we leaned our guns and listened to forest sounds and slapped at mosquitoes clotting our noses and ears.

The night was quiet and dewy and cold. A night bird cried and another called back.

Hamer's cigaret glowed inside his fingers. Time moved not at all, not even by the second.

Up came the sun.

How are the groceries holding out, Jordan called. I have eaten the stock off your rifle, Hinton said, and am starting on the barrel.

Along came Old Man Methvin in his jalopy, hollering that his boy might be with them and threatening federal heat.

So we chained him to a tree.

Then we waited some more.

hinton

alcorn

oakley

jordan

gault

hamer

Q. Please state your name.

A. Avie Methvin.

Q. What relation are you to Henry Methvin?

A. I am his mother.

Q. Do you know what arrangements were made for the ambush of those people by the officers?

A. Bonnie and Clyde you mean?

Q. When the plan was laid and sprung?

A. Yes.

Q. Were you present when you and your husband with the officers discussed the arrangements for their death?

A. Yes sir.

Q. What were the arrangements?

A. They told us they would give our boy his freedom. We told him we wanted to know if they would and they said, yes, they would.

Q. Tell the jury about it.

A. Well, the night they came they went on to Shreveport and Henry went with them and he went in to get some breakfast the next morning and got away from them.

MR. MASON: I move to strike the answer of the witness.

THE COURT: Sustained.

Q. Go ahead and tell the arrangements, if you know about them, yourself.

A. I was trying to tell it. Me and my husband went to Arcadia and so Mr. Joyner got word to them, and me and my husband went that night and told the sheriff what time they were to be back down there.

Q. What part did your husband play?

A. He was going to meet them to see if Henry was with them.

Q. What else?

A. He stopped them and some of the officers were out there hid when they came.

browning

winchester

winchester

remington

winchester

remington

Ted Hinton :

From the trees the butcher
birds stalked mice as Hamer
spit stars of juice in the dirt when,
singing like a sewing machine

in the distance, appeared a sight,
and coming on, topping the hill,
and then, driving down—on wings
of dust—

gathering form despite their speed,
appeared two figures, window framed.
Then they were on us and screaming,
and what happened

happened, and when I
open the door and she falls
into my arms, what hangs from
the frame is a bloody fringe.

When he woke again, it was lighter, the window fog was almost gone, and Bonnie had shifted so that she lay on her side, eyes shut in a soft manner, hands tucked between her knees. He resisted the impulse to pray until he saw her chest faintly rise at which he said a *thank you* in his mind. It was cold. He clamped his hands in his armpits and looked out at the chaos of branches and greenery. The leaves fluttered on their stems like fins wimpling on a school of fish. He leaned forward and placed his hand on Bonnie's stomach and kept it there for some time, then checked the 45 on the seat, the browning against his knee, and the shotgun in the floorboard. He pushed the ignition and pressed in the clutch and gas, and Bonnie opened her eyes.

It was an hour and a half before they made Gibsland, then they were riding that piney hallway south of town with a paper bag of sandwiches and a half sandwich of turkey and tomato from which Bonnie was subtracting hungry bites as they passed Buddy Goldston's logging truck with the swampers in back, and then they rolled down that straightaway hill into that hollow with the sweet gum trees and pine and bermed earth and the sun bearing down—and there it was, a sight so familiar they must've seen it a thousand times, Ivy Methvin's rattletrap truck, parked and facing them in their lane. A figure stepped out from behind it, waving them to a stop.

Clyde slowed.

It was the old farmer himself, approaching in his patchwork overalls. The man was tiny. He looked like two wires twisted together. His arms hung almost to his knees. He sidled up to Bonnie's window, all the while peering into the backseat.

Bonnie was mushing a bite. "Tire trouble?"

The old man waved generally at the truck. "This goddamn thing. Say, my boy aint with yall, is he? I come out looking for him."

Clyde cocked his head. "Now, why on earth would he be with us? Aint he come back to your place yet?"

The old man held his stomach and stepped back.

"What's wrong?" Bonnie said.

"I feel sort of puny," he said and hurried off into the brush.

The logging truck was bearing down, so Clyde shifted into first to pull out of the way. That's when Bonnie caught sight of movement in the trees—the torso of a man rising up with a rifle braced against his shoulder. A gunshot boomed. Clyde's head, caught fat in the left temple, snapped to the side as if he'd been mule kicked. His body, suddenly made of wicker, yawed toward her. The clutch jumped out from under his foot. Tires spat gravel. The morning flickered and receded and Bonnie saw the scene through the eyes of a gliding crow: a gray box churning dust along a brown strip, tiny puffs of smoke rising from the trees, the endless green all around—nothing of greater consequence than in any other fleeting scene, the lonely streets of a farm town or the lazy bend of a river.

Yet someone was screaming.

Then gunfire thunder and shrieking steel. A truck hit her in the face and shattered her teeth like glass. Another truck crashed into her shoulder. No, not trucks but a giant finger—making of her an insect with its clumsy jabs. The finger snapped her collarbone with a click. It insisted its nail into her neck. It flexed her chest until a rib bone buckled, then it bore through cartilage and rummaged around in her intestines as if feeling for a lost coin. It speared her thigh and nuzzled its tip up against her femur's long blade. She held up her right hand to catch, maybe, the fingertip and shove it aside, but her own fingers that had held that long ago cup of hot chocolate out to Clyde were flicked away as nothing much, leaves in a wind.

Ted Hinton was the first to emerge from the brush, and he stalked the Ford's back end, emptying one 45 and then another into it as it rumbled along, trailing a stack of dust. The other officers stepped down the bank and followed, firing. The car bumped off the road and trundled up into the bracken, where it whipped down long stalks of grass under its fender and folded over a sapling with a screech. When the car lurched to a stop against the berm, the dust stack sheared free and bucked into the air.

Hinton rushed into the crossfire. He crouched by the driver's side. As gunshots hammered cotton into his ears, he inched up his head and spied the driver an arm's length away. Clyde's neck stalk was limp, his head thrown back, his hair jackstrawed against the seat. A delta of blood swept from mouth to ear. Driving glasses with purple lenses hung under his chin, and the flat sheen of his eyes looked on the front windshield as a mist of red hit it. Clyde still clutched the 45 in his right hand—and there, through twisting dust and smoke, bunched against the passenger door, Hinton saw Bonnie, a child sized heap with her head pitched between her knees.

That's when Hamer walked up on Bonnie, leveled his 38 super with both hands, and put five shots through the window into her back.

Hinton waved off the firing, hollered, "For God's sake *stop*," but his voice vanished under the gavel raps of gunfire. The Ford's motor still purred and Hinton's mind conjured a grass fire, so he stood and squeezed his shoulders through the driver's window. Inside the car he heard cows bawling and saw sledgehammers driven into foreheads and trenches of gore, but somehow he closed his fingers over the key and turned off the machine and backed away. He gulped a few breaths of gunsmoke air, then placed a hand on the Ford's hood and bumped across it on his seat. It was this, his most careless act, that brought the firing of his fellow officers, finally, to a halt.

The passenger door handle felt cool on his palm. He pulled on it, and the woman who, during his long ago lunch breaks, used to serve him sandwiches and pie slices, who used to refill his coffee and tell of a bigger life on Broadway, who used to wink in that manner reserved only for him, this sparrow of a girl spilled into his arms.

She was as light and malleable as a child limp with sleep. Her body was warm, her face only recognizable in parts. On impulse, he held her under the arms and stood her up. She had come out of her shoes. The tips of her naked toes swept back and forth over the heads of sprung grass.

Bonnie :

Where was Clyde?

If she could be held in this man's arms and helped to standing, if she could yet draw breath, even though the both of them were shot to rags, filled full of holes, betrayed and injured on a backwater road, there must still be a single chance in a thousand that they could be tended and healed and find each other again and find the road and another afternoon of riding with the windows down, the trees flashing past—

Yesterday, parked outside the Shreveport cafe, a little girl in the car over pointed and said, Mama, see the lady smoking. The girl looked the same age Bonnie had been the summer a heat wave made the Dallas days unbearable. There was nowhere to go to escape the misery. Even nighttime brought no relief. Sweat pricked her scalp and ran down her arms in icy streaks. She and cousin Bess lay in the darkened back room and took turns fanning each other with a newspaper. If you could lie still, moving only your eyes, it was almost possible to believe that the heat would pass. Then, on a day when it seemed that the thermometer would boil over, that they all must melt away into puddles, her grandmother called her and Bess into the kitchen and set before each of them a plate with a slice of yellowmeat watermelon. Bonnie lifted the wedge, and when she put it in her mouth, she knew winter would again come. The melon was sweet and juicy and, above all, cold. She lingered over each bite, letting its coolness radiate out into her. After the first slice, there was another and another and another, and she and Bess must've taken an hour, just grinning and murmuring the whole time. When it was finished, she tilted the plate so the juices ran into her mouth. She was someone who'd tasted an icebox watermelon, she'd never told Clyde that—

Then the edges of things were fading. Spent embers crossed her vision trailing dark threads. Her inner fire fluctuated, at once persisting, at once relinquishing, which was the writhing fire of life itself, flashing then dying, seeking more grist, and, all the while, she was aware that the final guttering flash must come. What small light might be held and tended was, until that task was no longer hers. The longstanding fears fell away, and though she wasn't ready to be taken, death took her all the same.

Henderson Jordan :

I guess that I will never forget the sight of the inside of that car. It looked like where hogs had been slaughtered. In the lap of Clyde Barrow was a sawed-off 16-gauge automatic shotgun. His right hand was curled around the shortened stock. Seven grim notches had been carved in the wood by the killer. In Bonnie's lap was a .45 caliber automatic pistol. There were three notches on this gun. Between the pair was another automatic shotgun.

On the floor of the car was a bag containing forty clips for a Browning automatic rifle. Three rifles of that type were in the rear of the car. All were loaded. Under a robe on the rear seat were ten automatic pistols and one revolver, all fully loaded. Three bags and a box contained more than two thousand rounds of ammunition.

At the time of her death, Bonnie was wearing a red dress and red shoes. On Barrow's person was found more than five hundred dollars. The young killer was dressed in blue trousers and a white shirt. His tie, hanging on the rear vision mirror, had been shredded by bullets. Incidentally, he died with his shoes off.

Son, brother, lover. Ex con.

Daughter, wife, lover. Poet.

We talked our teacher into letting us get under the window and watch for them. And when we said, "Here they come," the whole school came out and blocked the street. They had no choice but to stop and let us see it. I ran and looked at Bonnie and her side of the car. Stuck my head in the window and looked. She had fallen forward. I could see her red hair and this rusty red dress she had on and see her back, and she looked like, through the shoulders, she couldn't have been over a foot wide. She was tiny. And there was a magazine on the floor there. Her hair was kind of lying on that.

And then I ran around to the other side and stuck my head in the car there and looked at Clyde, and someone jerked the blanket or whatever they had over his face. Well, I just remember his mouth was open, and, if I remember right, his eyes were, too. But you could tell that he was very dead.

It was, it was just gruesome.

—Mildred Cole Lyons

Clyde :

someone tugged me
up through roof
deep against gravity

whoareyou whoareyou

mans hedge a voice said
is his innocence
& in its absence

even goodness is dead

lifes dark comes first
it comes with birth
only death divines

whats behind the light

born blind one & all
then the hand let me fall

Bonnie :

The people of Bienville Parish knew us on sight. Clyde bought the Cole house by posing as an independent logger, but we were too well dressed to be a lumberjack and wife, they knew that. They sure nodded and said hello when they saw us, though. Tipped their hats and gave us free dinners. And when they heard the fusillade, they came from miles away. The dust had yet to settle when some of those same people carved off one of Clyde's fingers and a chunk of his ear, cut a lock from my hair and pieces off my dress. These souvenirs still decorate a mantel somewhere, I would guess.

In Arcadia it was a mob event. They had to spray the crowds with embalming fluid to keep them off our bodies. Our autopsies were done in the back of Conger's Furniture Store, where people in the swarm out front gouged bits from the tables and chairs to prove that they had been present at our demise.

The laws had been on our left side, and you'd think they were trying to impress someone. With four of six outside of jurisdiction, I suppose they wanted to be thorough. It didn't hurt that we'd never been tried in any court of law or found guilty of a single crime. Can you say judge, jury, and executioner? Forty shots just for me, not counting those that missed or the three I took in the head. As if that weren't enough, when the car bumped into the barrow pit, as you may witness here, one of them walked up alongside and shot me in the back:

> *3 parallel striking right side of back from base of*
> *neck to angular right scapula to side back bone,*
> *one striking midway back breaking back bone*

I claim no special favors for being a woman, but I was unarmed, sitting down, and enjoying my lunch, thank you very much. And another thing. Look at the coroner's loopy hand at the end of his report. It was all he could muster just to count the holes. Who's to say what he missed.

Buster Parker drove east to retrieve his sister's body

The dirty dogs did it from ambush he said

Did you see her

When Bonnie was three years old, the family was then attending Rowena Baptist Church—its services, business meetings, and box suppers—and each week Buster, who took great pride in his little sister, calling her "Blue" for her sapphire eyes, held her hand and promenaded with her the five blocks to Sunday School. One morning, a handful of pupils were selected to sing a cappella solos. The preacher sat behind them, smiling from the red velvet chair, his forefinger bookmarking the Bible in his lap.

The first soloist sang two verses from "His Eye Is on the Sparrow"; another, "Jesus Loves Me." When Bonnie's turn came, the Sunday School teacher patted her bottom, and the congregation watched the little girl in the yellow dress take the stage as if it were newly under her ownership. She pinched her dress by its hems and held her stance a moment too long. The Sunday School teacher nodded, then little Bonnie Parker pranced like an imp and belted out a honky tonk number she'd lifted off the radio:

He's a devil in his own hometown
On the level, on the level
He's as funny as a clown
He spends a five cent piece, thinks nothing of it
His pants all creased, red vest above it
And when it comes to women, oh! Oh! Oh! He ha!
He's a devil, he's a devil

An arctic wind blasted the sanctuary. Whispers rippled. Every eye hung on the preacher whose Adam's apple went into spasm. Buster's eyes crossed, and he buried his face in his mother's side.

Finally, the preacher stood, gathered himself, and with a wooden smile, invited the children to return to their seats despite two of the soloists not having had their turns. When the Parkers arrived back home for Sunday dinner, Buster announced to the household that, from there on out, someone else would have to see after his sister's religious education.

Emma Parker, her face covered with a handkerchief, leaves the funeral parlor after viewing her daughter's body. The two men holding her up are unidentified.

Clemmie Methvin :

I only saw them twice. I was pregnant with my oldest son and I had to be careful to keep from miscarrying. We were in the home of my brother-in-law one night when they came. They were like any other guest. I didn't really realize the danger we were all in.

The next time I saw them they came to our house just a week or two before the laws waylaid them and killed them. Bonnie was in the car drunk and when she was drunk she couldn't walk. She had been burned badly in a car wreck running from the laws. Clyde carried her into the house. They ate supper. I remember I had cooked home-cured ham and cornbread, I don't remember what else, but when they left Bonnie wanted to take the cornbread with her and some of it was in the car when they were killed.

The Bible says we reap what we sow. My father-in-law died a violent death. Someone ran over him with a car or someone beat him up and left him for dead. He didn't rally enough for the laws to get a statement from him, and my brother-in-law that was with Clyde and Bonnie supposedly was run over by a train. I can't believe anyone would crawl under a train to get to the other side. I believe someone pushed him.

Bonnie would have had a baby the same time I became a mother. I often count my blessings that my life has been different because of my Lord and Savior. The moral of this saga is it is better to live on bread and water than to have all the luxuries in the world, so when we lay down at night, we can sleep the sleep of a free person.

W. D. Jones : Final Fragment

*I run with Clyde and Bonnie for more than eight months.
That was all I could stand. I left them up in Mississippi
and hitchhiked back to Texas. The law caught me in
Houston. My running was over.*

*But it wasn't done yet. I had to pay. A boy in Houston,
where I was working for a vegetable peddler, knowed
me and turned me in to the law. They tried me for killing
a sheriff's man at Dallas. Clyde done it, but I was glad
to take the rap.*

*I've still got some lead in me from them fights with
the law. When I tried to join the army in World War Two
after I got out of prison, them doctors turned me down
because their X rays showed four buckshot and a bullet
in my chest and part of a lung blown away.*

*That Bonnie and Clyde movie made it all look sort
of glamorous, but like I told them teenaged boys sitting
near me at the drive-in showing: "Take it from an old
man who was there. It was hell."*

Bonnie :

Does chasing an endless road, dust and freeze ups, the blue skin burn of icy ditch waters, choking down the fat on a cold can of beans, shitting against a tire, pissing behind a tree, wiping yourself with leaves sound glamorous yet?

Them as has must lose 'cause them as hasn't can't, but that aint democratic, so they took our hearts and fed them bit by delicious red bit to the public to prove the one thing they'll never say, freedom don't pay.

Somewhere in the cave of space a star explodes.

AFTERWORD

It was my determination early on when deciding to pursue this story in a fictional manner to dispense with the type of primary research more fit to a purely historical investigation, yet I still wanted solid factual footing. Thanks to several historians, these competing impulses were reconcilable, and I'm indebted to John Neal Phillips, James R. Knight, Jonathan Davis, Boots Hinton, Ken M. Holmes Jr., Frank R. Ballinger, Jeff Guinn, Winston Ramsey, and Jan Fortune, among others. This novel found its central inspiration in their maintenance of the historical record.

At the same time, it must be admitted that the historical record is flawed. All history is error of some sort, and while discrepancies in any body of research are to be expected, they raise particular questions for historical fiction. Should one account's version of a disputed event (and, it should be noted, most major events in the saga of Bonnie and Clyde have multiple contradictory versions) be honored over another? A deeper tension lies in the bifurcated nature of the form itself, serving, as it does, two masters, history and fiction. In one sense, the best I can say is that this is my own error-riddled version of history, for, when it seemed necessary, I've added, subtracted, and distorted—an approach this note takes up in its conclusion. As well, my goal has never been an exhaustive cataloging of the couple's time together; such books already exist. It follows that a full bibliographical apparatus is unnecessary. But, in another sense, it *has* been my aim to draw as close as possible to the actual Bonnie and Clyde because doing so deepens the emotional connection. To change a story effectively, the teller must first know it intimately, and with dates and well-documented events, I've held this telling as close as possible to the known facts. It seems fitting, then, to note the main sources used.

Of those who rode with Bonnie and Clyde, we principally have Blanche Caldwell Barrow's *My Life with Bonnie & Clyde* (University of Oklahoma Press, 1994), assiduously annotated by Phillips; from her summaries in it (pp. 24-30; 112-17) are built the scenes at her stepfather's house and the Red Crown cabins in Platte City. W. D. Jones, trying to protect himself, gave a blatantly false "Voluntary Statement" to Dallas Police on November 18, 1933, but his "memoir" in *Playboy Magazine* (November 1968)—from which six fragments are excerpted—like Blanche's memoir, provides a convincing account of what it was like to ride with the couple day-in and day-out under both ordinary and extraordinary circumstances. From their other significant sidekick, Henry Methvin, and his mother Avie ("Ava" in the court records), we have their separate testimonies, also excerpted, from Henry's 1936 trial for the murder of Cal Campbell (*Methvin v. Oklahoma A-9060*). *The Truth About Bonnie and Clyde as Told by Billie Jean Parker*, an RCA Victor Recording from 1968, captures memories from an often-overlooked riding companion, Bonnie's sister. The reminiscences of Clyde's younger sister Marie, said to have ridden with them for short periods, are interesting in sentiment but problematic for the way she valorizes and defends Clyde and the factual errors she commits, working, as she is, with memories from a distant youth. The words of riding companion Joe Palmer about killing Major Crowson are composited from statements recorded in Phillips's *Running with Bonnie and Clyde* (p. 279, University of Oklahoma Press, 1996), as well as *Public Enemy Number One* (p. 78, Acclaimed Books, 1978), the memoir of Ray Hamilton's brother Floyd, who met with Bonnie and Clyde several times. Floyd is also interviewed in the 1968 documentary *Bonnie & Clyde: Myth or Madness*. Newspaper and magazine coverage that recounts the stories of kidnap victims, like Sophia Stone and Dillard Darby, but also Percy Boyd and Thomas Persell, give intimate glimpses as well.

A trove of primary material surfaced in 2010 when the FBI released, through its online vault, more than a thousand pages of files that document the efforts of its precursor, the Division of Investigation, to track Clyde Barrow and Bonnie Parker for seventeen months starting in January 1933. For the most part, this archive includes case reports and memos filed by field agents who were groomed in J. Edgar Hoover's detail-laden style. C. B. Winstead's memo noting Ray Hamilton's desire to kill Clyde appears on May 8, 1934; Hamer's handwritten memo about Bonnie's "delicate condition" appears on May 11, 1934; and R. Whitley's report about the need for a small group of officers to move "quietly and quickly" appears on May 14, 1934. In her poem "The Story of Bonnie and Clyde," Bonnie refers to "stool pigeons, spotters and rats," and the FBI files affirm the validity of the couple's fears, alluding to and sometimes identifying informants who were close to the couple and their families. Joe Bill Francis is never directly named as an informant; this is my deduction. For two weeks in April, 1934, the Dallas Police tapped the Barrow family phone, and a team of eavesdroppers recorded the conversations they heard in a 14"x6" daybook, which is kept in the Dallas Public Library archives. Nothing matches this source for giving a sense of daily life at the Barrow household and for capturing the family's microdialect. It also sheds light on the acrimony that developed between the Barrow and Hamilton clans. At one point, Cumie tells Emma, "I hope they catch Raymond and string him up right in front of Old Lady Hamilton," a curse that more or less came true when Ray was electrocuted in 1935.

From Bonnie's pen, we have diary entries from before meeting Clyde. "Why don't something happen?" she penned on January 11, 1928. We also have what amounts to a chapbook of poems, which includes her excerpted ballad. All the other poems in this book attributed to her and to others, except the poem by Cyclone Davis, are my inventions, as is Bonnie's journal entry dramatizing the Red Crown ambush, the format of which is modeled on Preston Sturges's movie scripts of the same period. Letters Bonnie wrote to Clyde while he was in prison survive, and some of his replies, less substantial, exist, clearly showing the pair's educational disparity. The letter to the *Houston Press* about where to find Wade McNabb's body (p. 295, *Ten Deadly Texans,* Daniel Anderson and Laurence Yadon, Pelican Press,

2009) is so well worded that it was likely written by Bonnie. In addition to Clyde's death insurance papers, The Bonnie & Clyde Ambush Museum in Gibsland, Louisiana, keeps, in a glass case, postcards that he penciled to his mother. Though the authenticity of the note to Henry Ford is disputed, Clyde's penchant for stealing Fords is unquestioned, and the sentiment, as well as some of its misspellings, are convincing enough despite his use of a false middle name; the original is on display at the Henry Ford Museum in Detroit. Other potentially authentic communiqués from Clyde include his letter of April 27, 1933, to Ray Hamilton while Ray was in the Dallas County jail; his letter to Amon Carter, editor of the *Fort Worth Star-Telegram*; and a note sent to Dallas Assistant District Attorney Winter King. There are a host of other signatures, cards, and letters bearing one or the other, and sometimes both, of the pair's imprints, including several guns carved with the initials "CB + BP" in museums and personal collections.

One source too readily dismissed by some historians is Jan Fortune's *Fugitives* (Ranger Press, 1934; Wild Horse Press, 2013), originally published just months after the fatal ambush. Compiled rapidly from interviews with Emma Parker, Nell Barrow, and others, sensationalized, and denounced by some family members because of Fortune's embellishing, it nevertheless contains minutiae of the couple's daily lives, family interactions, and a narrative of the moods Bonnie and Clyde experienced during their criminal run that continue to compel. Dialogue is, at times, taken directly from it, such as in the scene of Clyde's reunion with Bonnie after prison, in Buddy's memory of his Aunt Bonnie singing the crawdad song, and sporadically in the scenes of family meetings.

A hotly disputed point is Clyde's sexuality. Was he homosexual? Bisexual? Impotent? What does naming and categorizing such a thing as varied as human behavior tell us about a person anyway? What we can say for certain is that Clyde fiercely loved Bonnie. Yet his taking an apartment with Ray Hamilton, his repeated attempts to break Ray out of jail and prison, his willingness to risk everything to spring him from Eastham, his apparent desire to rejoin with Ray as late as March 1934, and his fierce denunciations of his old friend a month after their very public split, suggest that their relationship, whatever form it took, was also deeply felt. The photo of Clyde and Ray holding hands hangs in the Texas Ranger Hall of Fame in Waco.

Sheriff Schmid's scrapbook, kept in the Dallas Public Library archives, gives a sense of his desperation to end the pair's run. Ted Hinton's description of Bonnie at the café and his surprisingly lyrical account of the ambush come directly from his book, as told to Larry Grove, *Ambush* (Southwestern Historical Publications, 1979). The scenes in Sheriff Schmid's office are also drawn largely from his accounts, as well as discussions I had with Ted Hinton's son, L. J. (Boots). That Bonnie prostituted herself during her time as a Dallas waitress is a point of speculation in Jeff Guinn's book, *Go Down Together* (Simon and Schuster, 2009), that has angered her surviving relatives and been disparaged by many researchers. Part of the trouble is that Guinn commits a biographical fallacy when he bases this speculation on the content of Bonnie's poetry (Guinn, p. 111), but it's also clear that Bonnie came from a place and a social class not at all unfamiliar with prostitution, and, since accessing her inner life is central to this project, I've referred to the possibility of her considering such work only in a manner that matches her social environment and thinking as I came to know them.

It's untrue, as has been maintained at times, that the officers involved in the ambush kept mum for years as some sort of secret pact. Hamer, despite his legendary reticence, did speak with newspaper reporters at the time, and he gave a two-hour interview to Walter Prescott Webb on July 4, 1934, from which Webb constructs Hamer's first-person account of the ambush in *The Texas Rangers* (pp. 538-44, University of Texas Press, 1965). Henderson Jordan's account, "The Inside Story of the Killing of 'Bonnie' Parker and Clyde Barrow," as told to C. F. Waers, appeared in the November 1934, issue of *True Detective*. Drawn word-for-word from it are Jordan's account of selecting an ambush site and his description of the items found in the death car, including the clothes Bonnie and Clyde were wearing. Jordan's comparison of the car's interior to a hog slaughter is from his statement to H. Glenn Jordan on October 12, 1958, in the Texas Prison Museum files.

Also in the Texas Prison Museum archive is a copy of Clemmie Methvin's statement; she was Henry's sister-in-law who, pregnant herself in what would've been the same second trimester as Bonnie, seems a remarkably reliable firsthand witness to another woman's pregnant condition, decried as that possibility is in some quarters. Jimmy Mullen's signed statement of April 28, 1934 (found in the FBI files report made on May 3, 1934, by C. B. Winstead), includes Mullen's summary of a conversation with Mary O'Dare in which Mary criticized the couple's hygiene and "said Bonnie is pregnant, about six months." In addition, Special Agent Blake filed a report on May 22, 1934, that gives detailed information about the doctor in Ennis, Texas, who was treating Bonnie for her "pregnant condition," and it's this memo that links the epithet "delicate condition" to pregnancy. These reports of Bonnie's pregnancy appear in the record before the ambush and belie the claim that reports of her pregnancy arose as part of the apocryphal fog only after the couple's demise. They also prove that Hamer thought that Bonnie was pregnant at the time he shot her.

Lee Simmons's reminiscences are found in his memoir *Assignment Huntsville,* from which is also drawn dialogue between Hamer and Simmons. The article about Simmons's desire to give prisoners "more axes" is from the front page of *The Mexia Weekly Herald* on April 5, 1935. In *Running with Bonnie and Clyde* (p. 319), Phillips explains how Simmons's statement led to his resignation as prison manager. It should be noted, too, that in *Assignment Huntsville* (pp. 143-45), Simmons includes two letters to the Texas governor, signed by both himself and Frank Hamer, detailing the arrangements for Henry Methvin's Texas pardon.

For the manhunt itself and the portrait of its prime mover, Frank Hamer, the FBI vault holds some information. Sparing use is made of the hagiographical *I'm Frank Hamer* (Pemberton Press, 1968), which does, however, provide the substance from which the Remington company report is built, as well as Hamer's reminiscence about taking the job, including his claim that Bonnie and Clyde were the most dangerous criminals in American history. Hamer's boasts of extraordinary sensory powers are recorded by Webb in *The Texas Rangers* (pp. 523–24). Hamer's weaponry specifics are taken from Rick Cartledge's article "The Guns of Frank Hamer" in *OklahombreS* (spring 1993), which also provides Leslie Homer's take on the .38 Super. The graphic comic is a Stookie Allen original that I hired to be redone and altered by the British illustrator Gavin Ross. The news piece in which Hamer calls Bonnie and Clyde "murdering rats" and implies there were other murders that he committed as acts of personal retribution is a 1934 article by Archie B. McDonald, "Ace Man Hunter of Texas Says No. 1 Criminal of America Can Be Seized," in the Dallas Public Library files.

John Toland's spurious 1963 account of Bonnie and Clyde in *The Dillinger Days* (Da Capo Press) suffers from a narrow source base and a gullible adherence to W. D. Jones's false confession. The real era of Bonnie and Clyde historiography begins with Nelson Algren's introduction to the 1968 reissue of *Fortune's Fugitives*—this and the flood of renewed interest in the pair, of course, spurred by Arthur Penn's 1967 film *Bonnie and Clyde*. Algren's contextualizing of the pair within a larger narrative of exploitative greed, back-settler pride, abuse of policing powers, and the valorizing of the frontier outlaw made it possible to interpret the story in particularly American ways. Miriam Allen Deford's 1968 book *The Real Bonnie and Clyde* (Ace Books) is one of a handful of transparent attempts to capitalize on the film's popularity. Ted Hinton, the last living member of the fatal posse, left a valuable first-person record in *Ambush*, which was published posthumously in 1979. It was another five years before British author John Treherne set the criminal pair's story inside a psychoanalytical frame in *The Strange History of Bonnie and Clyde* (Stein and Day, 1984). Interest seems to have tapered off for a time, then in 2003, another British author, Winston Ramsey, along with a team of researchers, compiled the most thorough collection of historical artifacts to date for *On the Trail of Bonnie and Clyde Then and Now* (Battle of Britain). Knight and Davis's *Bonnie and Clyde: A Twenty-First Century Update* (Eakin, 2003) and Guinn's aforementioned book are similar in that they attempt comprehensive catalogs of the couple's exploits in narrative form. And the bedrock upon which all serious Bonnie and Clyde history stands is John Neal Phillips's research—in *My Life With Bonnie and Clyde, Running with Bonnie and Clyde*, and elsewhere.

Abuse Clyde endured at the hands of Dallas police is based on Floyd Hamilton's account of that force's interrogation methods (p. 23, *Public Enemy Number One*) and Phillips's interview with Mrs. John W. Hays, a friend of one of Clyde's girlfriends before Bonnie, in which Mrs. Hays states that the police would "beat him up and try to make him confess to things he'd never done" (p. 46, *Running with Bonnie and Clyde*). From the same book is drawn Ray Hamilton's last words and execution (pp. 278, 295-6). That J. Edgar Hoover would've flown to Iowa to personally interrogate a suspect such as Blanche Barrow is doubted by some historians. Nevertheless, the scene between the two is founded on her mention of just such a meeting in a 1984 interview with Phillips (Note 6, p. 289, *My Life With Bonnie and Clyde*); Knight and Davis give credence to this meeting as well (p. 114).

The extent and type of abuse Clyde suffered at Eastham is another contentious point, but Phillips's 1980 interview with Ralph Fults provides compelling evidence of the brutality both young inmates knew (*Running with Bonnie and Clyde*, pp. 49-54). I've further grounded this version, including the general conditions at Eastham, on the other contemporary texts noted above and on these sources: archived prison files in three locations—the Texas Prison Museum, the Texas State Library, which holds Clyde's and Buck's convict ledger records, and the Texas State Archives, which holds the Texas Prison Board Minutes from the era (Box 1998/038-8), monthly reports (Oversize 1998/257-2), and the inspection report from 1933 (Box 2002/027); Phillips's article "The Bloody 'ham," in manuscript form in the Dallas Public Library's archives; The Osborne Association's reports for the years 1932–37 (the "exceedingly black" conditions at Eastham are noted on p. 12 of the 1934 report; the excerpt from Sing Sing Prison Warden Lewis Lawes's address is on p. 18 of the 1937 report); Sid Underwood's *Depression Desperado* (Eakin, 1995); and Peter D. Tattersall's *Conviction* (Pegasus Rex, 1980). From his parole in February 1932, on, it's clear that Clyde sought to retaliate against Eastham for the treatment he endured there, but time and again until January 1934, his preparations were thwarted. In the end, it was necessary to assign Clyde a motivation for the act that precipitated his and Bonnie's end—namely, the prison raid—and, put simply, I chose his desire for retribution.

Reminiscences and other texts and their sources include: Troy Knighten, from Patrick McConal's *Over the Wall* (Eakin, 2000); Emma Parker, from *Fugitives*; Joe Palmer, from Treherne's *The Strange History of Bonnie and Clyde,* which also provides J. Edgar Hoover's statement about "convict lovers"; and Mildred Cole Lyons, from the 2007 documentary *Remembering Bonnie and Clyde.* The letter to Texas Senator Tom Connally is from Donald W. Whisenhunt's article, "East Texas and the Stock Market Crash" in the *East Texas Historical Journal.* Cyclone Davis's poem can be found in Whisenhunt's *Poetry of the People* (Popular Press, 1996). "Old Hannah," as sung by James "Iron Head" Baker, who was an inmate of the Central Farm Penitentiary near Sugarland, Texas, is from John A. Lomax's *Adventures of a Ballad Hunter* (Macmillan, 1947). Major Crowson's dying declaration is easily found, as is the *Ruffin v. The Commonwealth* ruling. The coroner's report excerpt is from Bonnie Parker's autopsy (Office of the Coroner of Bienville Parish, Arcadia, Louisiana).

For understanding the environmental degradation that precipitated the Dust Bowl, as well as the particular experiences of people living on or near the southern plains, sources abound. To name a few studies that were especially helpful, there are Thad Sitton and Dan K. Utley's *From Can See to Can't* (University of Texas, 1997); Donald Worster's *Dust Bowl* (Oxford University, 2004); Timothy Egan's *The Worst Hard Time* (Mariner Books, 2006), which provided the substance for the fabricated article about Black Jack Ketchum; Vance Johnson's *Heaven's Tableland* (Da Capo, 1974); William O. Douglas and Peter Parnall's *Farewell to Texas* (McGraw-Hill, 1967); and Dayton Duncan and Ken Burns's *The Dust Bowl* (Chronicle Books, 2012). Various articles in the *East Texas Historical Journal* also provide background information in this respect, including Mitchel Roth's article, "Bonnie and Clyde in Texas," from which is taken the quote about banks claiming to have been robbed by the couple as a badge of honor. "Dad" Joiner's story is drawn from my 2008 article "Dad Joiner's Dream" in *Oxford American* (pp. 42-49, no. 61). "There is no God west of Salina" is a refrain that reaches back to the Great Plains drought of the 1880s. "He was her man, but he done her wrong," is a line from the traditional song "Frankie and Johnny" but also a more particular reference to the 1933 film *She Done Him Wrong,* starring Mae West, which it's possible Bonnie and the Barrows saw during their hiatus in Joplin in April 1933. "Dungaree America" is largely a found poem, made up of lines from citizen letters during the Great Depression to Governor Miriam Ferguson, available in the Texas State Archives.

Clyde's fevered response in chapter 1, "Day by day in every way, I'm getting better and better," is a parroting of the 1920s mantra of pop hypnotherapist Émil Coué. The references to Jesse James, Billy the Kid, and the first and last stanzas of "The Execution of Wade McNabb" are included to acknowledge debts owed to this work's spiritual predecessors, Ron Hansen's *The Assassination of Jesse James by the Coward Robert Ford*, Michael Ondaatje's *The Collected Works of Billy the Kid,* and C. D. Wright's *Deepstep Come Shining.* For a novel to lean so heavily on poetry's powers is a matter of fitting container to content. "The poet has no place within the law," says Patrick Lane, and in drawing close to my subjects, it became necessary to stray into that most criminal of forms—that is, poetry.

To discuss, finally, the imperative for distortion, I'll readily admit that the couple in this story are very much my Bonnie and Clyde. The menu invented by Barrow gang hostage Sophia Stone is, for example, my own invention. From Billie Jean Parker, we know that there was often joking inside the car, and this moment allowed for some compensation on that score.

Not much is known about the gang's vacation to the southeast, and I exploited this gap in the record to give Clyde a fascination with sandcastles. The beach stopover posits aspects of Clyde's personality that, though fundamentally creative, had been stifled. On the other hand, a gap I chose not to explore along these same lines is Clyde's saxophone and guitar playing because, despite keeping instruments with him while on the run (his saxophone was found in the death car), so little is recorded about his skill level and musical preferences that speculation on this point risked a distortion too profound, for it would've been ongoing and not momentary.

As well, I've used this project to conjure my ancestors, providing, as it does, a chance to revivify the world and language of my paternal grandparents. Luther and Lillian (née Moore) Jones were, like Clyde, born to sharecroppers in east Texas during the same generation. They married two years before Bonnie and Clyde met and are, more or less, who Bonnie and Clyde would've become had the outlaws' families stayed in Rowena and Telico, their respective rural Texas birthplaces. Luther tried his hand at preaching and farming until acquiring a small plot of land. In the frenzy around Dad Joiner's discovery of oil, Luther—as the story goes—sold the mineral rights to the family land for a pittance; he was, family lore insists, swindled. Eventually, Luther settled in as the yard maintenance man of the nearby consolidated school for twenty-three years. Lillian was a schoolteacher who died giving birth to her second child, my father, in July 1934, the same month Bonnie would've had her child if the legend of her pregnancy is to be given credence (only a disinterment can answer this persistent question for certain). When creating dialogue, it was often family's voices I used as an authenticating standard.

Likewise, my maternal ancestry pressed its way in. Born in 1910, the same year as Bonnie and Clyde, my grandmother Vivian Daley was, as a teenager in northern Missouri one hot summer day, sitting with her girlfriend beside a well. The girls were dipping their necklaces in the cool water to help with the heat when a coupe roared past, then reversed, and the man driving stopped to offer a ride. This was my grandfather Russell Stephenson, whom my mother called Pappy, a man I know only as a figure in family stories since he died before I was born. Pappy was a fast-driving, lovable prankster with a penchant for drink, and I give what I know of his sensibility, including one of his favorite sayings, "Step on the gas and kick her in the ass," to Clyde.

How did those gaps in my own ancestry—never having known my father's mother and my mother's father—provide an imaginative space for this story? While I can't say for certain, it did provide an emotional connection to Bonnie and Clyde's generation and place, and it gave me, as well, a certain ownership and inventive freedom.

As for the Easter killings, though news reports at the time had Bonnie standing over and firing into H. D. Murphy's limp body, most Bonnie and Clyde historians now believe that it was Henry Methvin who performed this close-in execution, an interpretation based on several sources, including statements made by the closest eyewitnesses, Mr. and Mrs. Fred Giggal, who were in a passing car and whose accounts went underreported at the time. Historians also tend to agree that Clyde's intention, in ordering Methvin to "take them," was to kidnap the motorcycle officers, as he'd done with other lawmen on five occasions, and that Methvin, dulled by whiskey and misunderstanding the order, raised a Browning automatic rifle and killed E. B. Wheeler outright before firing on Murphy. The newspapers and Hamer and Simmons seized on the account of the other supposed eyewitness, farmer William Schieffer, who claimed to have seen the killings from his distant porch, though in later years, as his story grew in size, one version he offered had him crawling through the grass close enough to hear their voices. News reports also focused on the tragic death of Murphy, who was two weeks away from his wedding day. Regardless of who pulled the trigger, it was the Easter killings that finally, fully turned public opinion against Bonnie and Clyde, and one reason for manipulating the portrayal of these slayings is to suggest this changing sentiment.

Another invention is the meeting with Charles "Pretty Boy" Floyd, whose portrait is drawn from *The Life and Death of Pretty Boy Floyd* by Jeffery S. King (Kent State University, 1998) and *Pretty Boy* by Michael Wallis (W. W. Norton, 2011), the latter of whom states that Floyd never met the couple. Indeed, that such a meeting occurred is unproven, but Phillips determines, based on Cumie's unpublished memoirs and interviews with Marie Barrow, that the meeting did take place, as he writes in *Running with Bonnie and Clyde* (p. 139). Knight and Davis also note that a meeting is possible (p. 91). None of these sources suggest what may have been discussed during such a meeting, so I used this blank spot for some revelations, including that Bonnie and Clyde shared a venereal disease, which is a claim that was made by the ambuscading officers and the coroner's jurymen after the ambush, according to Carroll Y. Rich's 1970 article "The Autopsy of Bonnie and Clyde" in *Western Folklore*. "Petty cutpurses" is a gibe traditionally attributed to Bonnie and Clyde not by Floyd but by John Dillinger.

"The Execution of Wade McNabb" posits McNabb's corpse being dropped in a well, though his body in reality was found—by following the map drawn on a piece of cardboard and mailed to the *Houston Press*—on a small rise, facedown with his head inside his hat and his hands crossed in front of him. That Henry Methvin mailed the map is imagination, and the invention of a well without bottom is a poetic necessity. In Clyde's ruminations on prayer, I assign an episode from Joseph Stalin's boyhood—lying in wait for an enemy with a board in hand—to Clyde, a conflation justified by the striking similarities in their megalomaniacal personalities as well as their grudge-driven obsessions with physical retributive justice.

The title is a distortion of Francesca's words, *Amor condusse noi ad una morte*—"Love gave us both one death," as translated by Robert Pinksy—to Dante in *The Inferno* when he enters the realm of carnal sinners. It's her explanation of the fate she shared with her adulterous lover, Paolo. Altering the verb form allows the title to stand not only as a statement of fact within the dialect of the dispossessed southerner, but also as a mortal plea addressed to Eros.

The final chapter title "Death on Ringgold Road" provides the closing example. "Ringgold Road" designates the highway along which Bonnie and Clyde were killed in a manner more consistent with music than actuality. Though the death road did lead to the town of Ringgold, the modern-day Highway 154 was, in 1934, known as the Sailes Highway. "Death on the Sailes Highway," however, not only fails to attain alliterative pleasure, but it misses poetic ambiguities embedded in the interplay of the syllabic transition in "Ringgold." Where does the guttural occlusion occur and what does it suggest? Is it reen gold, a furrowed ushering into glory, or ring old, a timeless tale of the death we all must face?—a provocation on which this note ends.